THE DARK CURTAIN

Joy Packer's new novel is a vivid blend of romance and adventure. Ruthless daring is matched by steadfast faith: individual courage and reason are pitted against the dark forces of violence and witchcraft.

Maud Carpenter, 62, world-famous thriller writer and mother-in-law to Sir Hugh Etheridge, British Ambassador in South Africa, disappears without trace when on safari in a wild life reserve: her family are confronted with a crisis. A ransom demand, gruesomely delivered, at first suggests a politically motivated kidnapping. But soon it becomes clear that the motivation of the kidnappers is more complex. . . .

also by Joy Packer

NOVELS

Valley of the Vines
Nor the Moon by Night
The High Roof
The Glass Barrier
The Man in the Mews
The Blind Spot
Leopard in the Fold
Veronica
Boomerang

AUTOBIOGRAPHY

Pack and Follow
Grey Mistress
Apes and Ivory
Home from Sea

TRAVEL

The World is a Proud Place

BIOGRAPHY

Deep as the Sea

Joy Packer

The Dark Curtain

Eyre Methuen London

First published 1977 by
Eyre Methuen Limited
11 New Fetter Lane
London EC4P 4EE

ISBN 0 413 37140 9

Photoset, printed and bound
in Great Britain by
Redwood Burn Limited
Trowbridge & Esher

Thank you, Caroline. And Bob too, and Camilla, Joanna and Emma, who all helped in their separate ways.

Joy

AUTHOR'S NOTE

There is no country in Southern Africa, nor anywhere in the Third World, called Nyangreela, and all the characters in this novel are equally fictitious. Any resemblance to any individual, living or dead, is purely incidental.

JOY PACKER

1977

1

'Don't speak of her in the past tense!'

Of the five people on the terrace of the British Embassy in Cape Town that summer night Kim Farrar was the only one who could see the problem objectively. The other four were too closely involved. He was the stranger – the war correspondent from the lacerated African lands beyond South Africa's border, whose articles were syndicated in many languages and whose personality was well-known on television.

Desmond Yates, the Second Secretary, had met him at the airport a few hours earlier when the fast flight from Johannesburg landed in Cape Town.

'Kim Farrar?' Yates had easily picked the tall loose-limbed figure in bush-jacket and shorts out of the crowd of summer visitors. 'I've seen you often enough on the box to recognise you. I'm Desmond Yates, Second Secretary. The Ambassador is expecting you to spend the next few days at the Embassy.'

'That'll be fine. I guess there's a red-hot story waiting for me on the doorstep.'

'A very unfinished story. The Ambassador's mother-in-law, the red-hot heroine, is still in limbo. Give me your hand-gear and grab the rest of your stuff off the conveyor-belt. It's just coming up.'

'There it is – that canvas kit-bag. I travel light.'

Farrar had followed Yates to his Mercedes Sports with a C.D. number. The sun was warm but a strong south-easter blew his thatch of dark hair wildly about his head and ruffled his companion's fair rather close-cropped curls. Yates walked with a brisk athletic stride and Farrar thought the Second Secretary did not quite fit the conventional notion of a cultured diplomat, dabbling in intrigues and trained to believe that the pen was mightier than the sword. Culture young Yates might have, and a fancy for intrigues of all sorts but he was clearly a man of action – just as well in an era when diplomats were high priority targets for terrorists. Diplomatic privilege had become precarious.

Clear of the airport, Yates had disregarded the speed limit. Table Mountain and Devil's Peak rushed towards them.

'You'll have a couple of hours to sort yourself out,' he'd said. 'There are messages waiting for you at the Embassy and a direct-line telephone in your room. The Ambassador is engaged till seven-thirty when we'll meet for an informal family dinner – and a discussion.'

'Family?'

'The Ambassador and Lady Etheridge, and Jane Etheridge. Jane is Sir Hugh's daughter. Her mother died when she was a kid, so Mabel – the present Lady Etheridge – is her stepmother.'

'So our famous captive, Maud Carpenter – queen of the fiction world and murder in a homely setting – is Jane Etheridge's grandmother?'

'Right. And they're rather alike in many ways – headstrong, impulsive and impatient.'

'What do I wear? I've only brought essentials.'

Yates had an infectious laugh. 'Not to worry. I can lend you anything you need. We're about the same height. And the moment you step into the Embassy hall the butler, Elias, will grab your belongings, unpack them and see that everything washable or pressable gets full and instant treatment. Besides, I can assure you that when H.E. says "informal", he means it. With him there's no middle course. He likes total informality or the full ceremonial. And, by the way, when he fixes you with a mesmeric eye and utters not one word, don't lose your head and break in. Just wait for it. Most people panic, but I fancy you don't panic easily.'

'You fancy right. But it's a help to be forewarned. I gather H.E. is co-operative with the press.'

'He plays ball with all the media, but he expects a comeback. He'll want to pick your brains and get you to use your sources to help find his mother-in-law, Maud Carpenter.'

'A far better assignment than most I've had recently!'

'Here we are – on Snob's Hill – as lovely a setting as you'd wish to find, and a swimming-pool in the garden. It's fairly protected from the south-easter and you'll have it to yourself this afternoon. Jane and Lady Etheridge have gone to a wedding and I'll be in attendance on H.E. till dinnertime. D'you think you'll need anything –'

'No thanks. I can manage reputable, informal rig with Elias's help.'

Yates nodded and glanced at the visitor. He reckoned that Kim Farrar was about due for a taste of civilisation. He'd lived on a diet of guerilla warfare, atrocities, overcrowded refugee camps steeped in sickness and despair for months. Little wonder the guy was skinny as a wild lizard-eating tom-cat.

Kim having consumed crayfish cocktail, a tender tournedos, rum soufflé, cheese and fruit, and enjoyed the sherry and wines of the famous Cape vineyards – now relaxed on the terrace, a liqueur brandy at his side as he smoked one of his host's Havanas.

Elias removed the coffee-tray, replaced it with drinks and glasses, and bowed a polite goodnight. So at last the two young men and the family were alone.

The Ambassador, Sir Hugh Etheridge, was grey-haired and

grey-eyed, with fine features and an air of breeding as clearly defined as that of the string of horses carrying his racing colours past the post in England, Ireland or South Africa. His wife was agreeable and elegant. She had strong blunt hands, noted Farrar. Practical. The girl, Jane, was tallish, supple and graceful. Her shoulder-length hair was as dark as his own and her eyes, in the dim light of the terrace, seemed night-black under thick lashes. Her tan was deep and even.

Five of us here, Farrar reflected, clean and comfortable, but dominated by the absent sixth – Maud Carpenter, who might be imprisoned anywhere, and whose name had not even been mentioned during dinner.

'One has to be discreet in front of the staff,' Lady Etheridge explained. 'Every word sparks off a new rumour. I can't describe what it's been like – everything from terrorists to wild beasts and even wilder suggestions.' She shuddered. 'You know what happened, of course, Mr Farrar?'

'Kim, please.' He flashed her his pleasant smile and answered her question as best he could. 'Roughly, yes. I know Mrs Carpenter was kidnapped from a Game Sanctuary some three weeks ago, but I was too out of touch to get the full follow-up or any details.'

Sir Hugh intervened. 'I'll fill those in for you presently. But first tell me if you've ever met my mother-in-law. Quite a formidable personality, though engaging in her way.'

The south-easter had dropped to a light breeze, carrying the summer scents and sounds of the starlit garden to the terrace above – frangipani, jasmine, tobacco-flowers, the rustle of oak and magnolia leaves, croaks and plops from the lily-pond, the forlorn cry of a night bird; while, high on the shoulder of Devil's Peak, the heavy white wind-cloud was fraying and dissolving, gradually revealing the granite buttresses and forested gorges of the southern aspect of Table Mountain. At its feet the lights of the city and the bay spread their shimmering web northward to the ranges guarding the hinterland.

'As a matter of fact, yes,' said Kim. 'Mrs Carpenter and I happened to be fellow-passengers on the flight from Heathrow to Johannesburg some months ago. She had a good deal of hand-luggage – a camera, a portable typewriter, a tape-recorder and so on. I helped her carry it from the plane. She astounded me by talking Afrikaans to the customs officers. We had no trouble after that!'

'She was born and bred in South Africa,' Sir Hugh remarked. 'But, as you probably know, she's addicted to London and the countryside. Her husband was an English landowner and English village life became the setting for most of her novels.'

'She made crime so cosy,' sighed Lady Etheridge. 'That was the secret of her success, of course. Poison at the rectory – delicious –'

'Don't speak of her in the past tense!' flared Jane. 'I can't stand it.'

Sir Hugh ignored his daughter's outburst and turned to Kim. 'You were saying . . . ?'

'Mrs Carpenter and I both had to wait for connections at Jan Smuts Airport. So we had coffee together, and rather an odd conversation considering we were strangers to each other.'

Mabel Etheridge arched an interrogative eyebrow. 'Hardly strangers. A famous novelist and a well-known T.V. personality. All the same, I can guess who did most of the talking.'

Farrar said with a sympathetic grin, 'Mrs Carpenter is a very positive personality, with strong views.'

'And this odd conversation,' Sir Hugh prompted. 'Could it have any bearing on the present situation?'

'As for the present situation, I've not yet been fully briefed, sir. But Mrs Carpenter told me that after her husband's death she had felt the need for change and solitude – for a safari – and, as she put it, "the innocence of wild animals". She seemed obsessed with the idea that too many people in too little space were turning humans into savage beasts in a rather horrible way.'

'People are basically beasts – *plus*!' put in Jane. 'Because they have the ability to think, they manipulate instinct and corrupt it. Real animal behaviour is predictable – in accord with nature's laws.'

Sir Hugh made a sign to his daughter and she turned to Farrar with a quick apologetic shrug.

'Sorry, Kim. Carry on.'

'That was what your grandmother reckoned, Jane. She had plenty to say about scientists – good and evil – but the main targets of her wrath were the political killers who work in packs like wild dogs.'

'Did she make constructive suggestions for controlling hi-jacking, kidnapping, bomb-planting – the massacre of innocents as a means to a dubious end?' asked the Ambassador, whose mother-in-law had frequently irritated him by her assumption that she had all the answers.

Jane's eyes were on Farrar. In the pause that followed, his face had hardened and he seemed older than she'd thought at first. Thirty? Thirty-five?

'Mrs Carpenter is all for Israel's attitude where hi-jacking is concerned. Wherever possible, force should be met by force and cunning matched by cunning, plus daring. Hi-jackers should be shot without mercy.'

'At whatever the cost to the hostages?' demanded Yates.

'Mrs Carpenter admitted it was hard on the sacrifices, but that giving in to terrorist demands could only result in the escalation of violence.'

Mabel Etheridge said quietly, 'She's right, of course. As things go these days, terrorists are fanatics who regard themselves as martyr material – like their victims. We live in a world of gangsters. All sorts.'

'What about kidnapping?' asked Yates.

'She reckoned the victim, if possible, should refuse to be used as bait by blackmailers and extortionists.'

The wind had ceased to breathe, intensifying the oppressive silence that followed Farrar's words. The Ambassador's eyes were fixed on the journalist's face. When he spoke it was with the deliberation Jane knew so well.

'Well, seeing that fate arranged your inadvertent meeting, you can assess our predicament more accurately. You've seen and heard for yourself how intractable Mrs Carpenter is – an individualist impervious to advice or argument when her mind is made up.'

Farrar stubbed out his cigar carefully. He was conscious of Jane watching him intently, waiting for his answer.

'With respect, sir, I didn't get that impression.'

'You surprise me.'

'I think it's Mrs Carpenter who could surprise any of us. As you say, she holds strong views and principles, but her mind isn't closed to suggestion. She's a good listener. When one talks to her she isn't just thinking of what she's going to say next, she's giving the opposition careful consideration. Then she slaps it down. Or modifies her own attitudes.'

Jane sprang to her feet. 'Of course! Gran is logical and flexible. But how can we tell what attitude she's taking in her own case when we haven't heard a word from her kidnappers? That's what's driving us mad. The awful silence! Not knowing where she is or who's got her.'

Kim turned to the Ambassador. 'Could you let me have the whole sequence of events in chronological order?'

'Of course. The supposed kidnapping, or possible accident or even murder, received great publicity at first, and then – as happens when no solution is forthcoming – it was dropped by the media and you, till now, were in no position to follow up the story.'

Sir Hugh settled back and addressed himself exclusively to Farrar.

'A month ago Mrs Carpenter decided to join a safari organised by a private company which is developing a promising Wild Life Reserve not far south of the Mozambique border. I pointed out that this particular park was not yet sponsored by South African tourism and that no safe border existed in Africa today. In order to join the tour she planned, she would have to sign a form stating that she did so at her own risk.' He paused and turned to his wife. 'You heard her answer, Mabel.'

Lady Etheridge agreed emphatically. 'She was insufferable. She said, "I may be your house-guest as well as your mother-in-law, Hugh, but I'm over sixty and not yet in my dotage. If I want to take a normal tourist risk I shall do so with, or without, your permission."'

Desmond Yates, who had also witnessed this small rebellion against the Ambassador's authority, stifled an impulse to laugh. Instead he remarked, 'Mrs Carpenter said it very amiably.'

Mabel Etheridge threw him a reproachful glance.

'Amiably, but forcefully. And she knew very well that her value as a kidnap proposition was far above the normal tourist risk. A thriller-writer whose books are dramatised and filmed and bring in a fortune! She was asking for trouble.'

'And got it, unfortunately.' Sir Hugh made a sign to his daughter. 'As you seem restless, Jane, you might bring me a whisky and water. Desmond, look after my wife, and Kim and yourself. Elias will have left everything on the trolley.'

When they had settled down once more the Ambassador

resumed his account.

'As you probably know, Kim, the Safari-Coach party – about a dozen assorted British and American tourists – arrived at Marula Grove a week after leaving Cape Town. The Sanctuary is a few kilometres inside the north-eastern border of the Republic in beautiful and romantic scenery. But the set-up is fairly primitive as yet – a few thatched rondavels in a semi-circle round a camp kitchen and open grill. Only lamps and torches. The sanitation is limited to a couple of earth loos, like rough sentry-boxes, some distance from the living quarters and placed just inside the thorn stockade which encloses the camp. And that was where Mrs Carpenter disappeared on the night after their arrival.'

'Pity there weren't any sentries about,' murmured Mabel Etheridge. Her husband waved away the interruption.

'From dusk to dawn the main gates are locked and no visitor enters or leaves the fenced perimeter. Mrs Carpenter, of course, was given V.I.P. treatment – a rondavel to herself. You probably know the area, Kim. Long, thick grass, patches of dense bush, a river infested by crocs and hippos, a wealth of game of every variety, predators to hunt it, vultures to share it, flocks of glorious birds, a few rhinos, giraffe and elephant herds.'

'I've been there, sir. A paradise for game – also for poachers.'

'Or other evil doers! Well, the party followed the usual drill on the first day. Out at dawn with a game-ranger, rest during the noon heat when the game lies up, and out again towards evening when the animals assemble at the various water-holes. That night, the inevitable camp-fire, barbecue, sing-song and so to bed. During the small hours of the night Mrs Carpenter got up, pulled on a pair of khaki slacks and moccasin-type veld-shoes, and was observed by an American tourist, as she walked down the path from her rondavel to the loo, the torch-light bobbing ahead of her. He thought nothing of it and turned in. That was the last anyone has seen of her to our knowledge. All we know for sure is that the fence was breached just there and Mrs Carpenter's torch was found lying on the disturbed ground inside the blockade, also one moccasin and remnants of bloodied khaki material. There were wisps of hair in the thorn fence aperture, clearly hers – fair turning grey – but outside the fence the grass is high and thick with bush beyond it, and though someone appeared to have been dragged through it, no spoor could be traced. A heavy shower at about four a.m. had seen to that.

'She was found to be missing when her early morning tea was taken to her. The nightguards were interrogated. They were blank and silent as only an African can be when he wants to keep his tongue safely in his head, though they agreed with Travers, the ranger in charge of the camp, that some large animal had "clawed" its way through the fence. Travers, a reliable fellow, swears that he inspects the stockade every evening so one can only assume that it was deliberately breached after nightfall. It was a moonless night and the preliminary job could have been done during the sing-song.'

Farrar said: 'With the connivance of a campguard, no doubt. What about the South African anti-terrorist patrols stationed between Marula and the river border?'

'They are always on the lookout for evidence. But it's a very long border and a month has elapsed since Maud's disappearance. So I'm afraid all our information is negative.'

'Not *all*, Daddy. There are rumours you tend to discard.'

Jane faced her father tensely. Farrar's gaze shifted questioningly from the Ambassador to his daughter. She turned to meet the journalist's eyes, her own darkly defiant.

'Three days ago our Scottie, Kirsty, came into season and I took her to kennels. When I got back here Elias met me and said, "Now we have no watchdog, Miss Jane." He looked upset. I said, "She'll be back in three weeks. Why do you bother?"'

She paused. Her long slender throat was working.

'Please go on,' said Farrar. 'Everything could be important, every remark, however trivial.'

'Elias told me there was "talk that Leopard-Men had been near the place the old Madam was lost". He was frightened. When I tried to pump him, he shut up. He seemed to reckon he'd said too much already.'

Farrar nodded. 'If he believed the rumour he had reason to be scared. The Leopard-Men belong to a cult which creates fear – human beasts with ferocious masks, steel claws and strange powers and rituals. Two things puzzle me. If Mrs Carpenter was seized by a wild animal she would surely have been heard to scream. Night in the bush is very quiet – only its own sounds. Again, if an animal had taken her, something would have been found –'

Jane faced him. 'Of course. Bones, human bones! In spite of the vultures, the scavengers and the ants – *something* would have remained.'

Her agitation moved him to say, 'Don't you see, Jane, the very fact that no such evidence has been found is reason for hope?'

'If it was a snatch we'll get her back,' put in Yates. 'And Kim is right, Jane. Everything points to kidnapping.'

'But the Leopard-Men, Desmond?'

'That story has been put about to intimidate the Blacks. Anyone who has information or a theory will keep it to himself with a possible Leopard-Man breathing down his neck.'

Lady Etheridge covered her eyes with her hands, and the Ambassador carefully relit his half-smoked cigar. Yates seized the opportunity to put an arm about Jane's shoulders for a moment and she seemed glad of the comforting contact.

Even the Embassy garden appeared sinister now. Devil's Peak, clear of its last wind clouds, stood against the stars, powerful, dark, as if its forested slopes and naked crags were holding some silent potent warning.

'If Mrs Carpenter is still alive,' said Sir Hugh, 'some demand for ransom will come to me personally. And soon.'

Jane got up restlessly.

'Anything would be better than this suspense – ' She broke off with a gasp and drew back, her hand over her mouth.

Desmond ran forward to catch the man who stumbled, gasping and incoherent, up the steps to the terrace.

2
'Very special gloves!'

The Ambassador was shaken out of his habitual calm as he recognised the injured man.

Elias was ashen grey, his eyes bulging, his shirt and trousers blood-soaked and ripped to show the long deep triple gashes on his left arm and thigh. Without Desmond's support the man would have collapsed.

'Elias, what the devil has happened to you? Where is Sam? We don't keep a night-watchman as an ornament!'

Elias, in shock, mumbled something inaudible. Yates helped him onto a chaise-longue and Farrar went to the drinks trolley and poured a brandy which he held to the lips of the man fast lapsing into unconsciousness.

'Mabel,' said Sir Hugh. 'Bring the first-aid kit and a bowl of hot water.' He turned to his daughter. 'Ring Dr Grobbelaar, Jane, and ask him to come at once. If you can't get him at home use the emergency number and get hold of whoever happens to be on duty. There's no time to be lost.'

The butler was showing signs of revival and for a long moment the Ambassador considered the recumbent figure. Then he addressed Yates, his questioning glance including Farrar.

'The police?'

'Not just yet, sir.' Yates answered with decision. But the word 'police', combined with the brandy, brought a strong reaction from the injured butler.

'No police, Excellency! He kill me if police come hunt him.'

'Who'll kill you?'

Elias shuddered. 'The Leopard, Excellency – the Leopard-Man.'

Farrar knelt by Elias and tore the already shredded material from the bloodied arm to reveal the full extent of the vicious gaping claw marks from shoulder to elbow. The man's skin was cold and clammy, his pulse feeble.

'This ripper job is the work of a Leopard-Man all right,' said Farrar. 'From thigh to knee also. The wound'll need stitching. But I agree with Yates. To enlist the police before you know the full story – or as much as Elias dares to tell us – could invite his certain death.'

Lady Etheridge came onto the terrace with a first-aid tray. She placed it on a low table beside the chaise-longue. Lips compressed, she took charge.

'Jane, will you help me now?'

She cut away the entire sleeve and trouser-leg and told Jane to put them on one side. 'They may be needed as evidence.' She added to Elias, 'I'm not going to hurt you. His Excellency's own doctor will make you well. These things I have here are only in case he should need them. Can you tell us exactly what happened? Where is Sam?'

Jane, suppressing nausea, helped her stepmother slide clean towels under the injured limbs. How pink and raw the oozing wounds looked under the black epidermis! Skin deep, she thought, just one thin layer between Black and White. Or is it a whole world of atavistic superstition like Leopard-Men and rituals beyond our powers of imagination? Come to that, if some jungle creature, man or beast, could do this to Elias, what of her grandmother? Inside the house a clock struck midnight.

It was Lady Etheridge, gently swabbing the wounds, who discovered the paper in the shirt pocket. She withdrew it and passed it silently to her husband. He placed it, unread, in his clean white handkerchief and tucked it with fastidious reluctance into the pocket of his tropical jacket. He leaned over the butler and spoke to him with his usual clear deliberation. 'Now try to tell me exactly what happened.' He had to bend his head close to the man's lips to hear his faltering words.

'I am sleeping, Excellency. There is great knocking on my door and Sam shouting "Come out!" I hear the fright in him, so I call "Why? What thing is wrong?" He shout "There is wild animal!" I pull on some clothes and open up, but Sam rush away, frightened. I take big stick and torch, I hear grunts close by the hedge, I see the Leopard.' Elias shuddered. 'He stand on two legs and jump at me. He knock my stick away, I feel his claws. He growls. I know now I must die.'

'What saved you?' asked Farrar briskly.

The butler's eyes rolled in his deathly grey face. 'Leopard-Man want messenger. My arm, my leg burn like fire, I smell my own blood. He push something in my shirt-pocket, he say "Give your master this writing or Leopard-Man come again to finish you."' Elias made an effort to reach for the paper.

'It's all right,' said Farrar. 'Your master has the writing. You won't die. You're safe here. What language did this Leopard-Man speak? Xhosa –'

'He speak Fanagalo.'

Farrar turned to Sir Hugh. 'That's no language – just the bastard Esperanto of the mines, of Africa from the Cape to the Equator. No clues there.'

The sound of a car swept into the drive.

'Dr Grobbelaar, thank God!' Lady Etheridge hurried to the heavy front doors.

Suddenly Jane found herself alone on the terrace with her father and Elias, who had lapsed once more into semi-consciousness. She pushed her hair back from her forehead and her brow furrowed.

'I don't understand your delay in calling up Colonel Storr. He's our contact here – the head of the Peninsula Murder and Robbery Squad. So surely it's our duty. Even if it were nothing to do with Gran's kidnapping – which is most obviously is – it's a cruel assault.'

He touched the soft fall of his daughter's hair with a rare demonstration of affection.

'There are two things I want first. Dr Grobbelaar's report and time to examine and analyse this demand for ransom.' He indicated his jacket pocket. 'Then we should know where we stand.'

'Should, yes – but will we? Does one ever in a hostage case? Like blackmail, it goes on and on. Like that poor archaeologist in the Sahara. The ransom was paid but it took three years to get her released.'

Within the hour Colonel Storr was in charge. He took statements from everybody concerned, including Sam, the night-watchman, who met all questions with blank silence. He had seen and heard no evil and spoke none. Even Elias, his wounds cleansed and stitched, and back in his own bed, appeared to be suffering from amnesia. 'I don't remember,' was all he could mutter.

A lusty police guard with a well-trained Alsatian was stationed outside the staff quarters.

'The police are here for your protection,' Yates told Elias. 'You've delivered the message. You've nothing more to fear.'

Elias rolled his eyes wildly when the constable introduced him to the Alsatian. 'See this dog, man! Hunter by name and hunter by nature. If your bloody leopard comes back, Hunter'll fix him. He'll chase him, catch him and eat him up from whiskers to toenails.'

'What leopard?' asked Elias faintly and turned his face to the wall.

In the drawing-room Dr Grobbelaar reassured the Ambassador and his family as he took his leave.

'Your man will be all right. Those claw-wounds were ripped by steel, I'd say. *Very* special gloves! All the same I've given him an anti-tetanus injection. I'll pop in tomorrow and if there's any sign of infection we'll whip him off to hospital. Meanwhile I'm prescribing bed and a sedative for Lady Etheridge. Right now.' He turned to Colonel Storr. 'Hope you get your man – or should I say your leopard?'

'We will,' growled the burly Police Chief. 'Man or beast – or both. And now I must be going too.'

As Yates walked to their cars with the doctor and the Colonel, Jane took her stepmother's arm.

'Come, Mabel. You look all in.' But, as they left the room, she said, over her shoulder, 'I'll go up with Mabel, Daddy, and tuck her up. Then I'll be back.'

Alone in the drawing-room with Farrar, the Ambassador stood in his customary attitude by the fireplace, hands loosely locked behind him.

'You want to know if news and details of the ransom demand are for release,' he said. 'My answer is: *Not at present*. The demand is outrageous and will have to be dealt with at a high political, diplomatic and personal level. Meanwhile you can take this photostat of the letter, but I must have your assurance that you will regard it as top secret till I give you the all clear. You can discuss it with Desmond Yates, if you wish. No one else.'

Sir Hugh had used his influence to recruit Farrar as his liaison with the media. Few T.V. interviewers or newsmen knew Africa as Farrar did and fewer still had both diplomatic experience and a reputation for discretion and integrity. Of course the Carpenter case had the makings of a first-class scoop, and possibly a book, so it was all to Farrar's advantage to keep inside information to himself until the story was ripe to break. The moment the Ambassador had met Farrar he had been favourably impressed. Already he regarded the journalist as an ally.

Later, when Kim and Yates had gone, Sir Hugh went down to the terrace, already washed down by Sam, who had sheepishly returned to duty and was reluctantly doing his rounds, *knopkierie* in hand. The presence of the policeman and Hunter did nothing to reassure him. How did he know that the Alsatian would not mistake him, Sam, for a Leopard-Man?

The Ambassador stood staring into the garden. Inwardly, he cursed his mother-in-law for the trouble she had brought upon herself and her family. Why did Maud always have to take her own line regardless of anybody's advice?

He turned as light footsteps crossed the long drawing-room and Jane came through the French doors and tucked her arm in his. The confiding gesture warmed his heart and for a moment it seemed to him that a perceptibly growing rift between them had narrowed. She always took her grandmother's side against him and he resented it, just as he guessed she resented her stepmother.

'Mabel's in bed, drowsy already,' she said. 'I know you've had about all you can take, Daddy, but I *have* to see the ransom demand for myself.'

'Of course, Janie. Colonel Storr took the original but left me some photostats. Let's go indoors now. It's grown cold – or seems so because we're tired.'

While her father locked the French doors and closed the slatted shutters, she curled up on the couch under the reading-lamp to study the photostat he had given her.

To her surprise she saw that the dictated letter had been written in her grandmother's own unmistakable scrawl.

Send Yates *alone*, early passenger flight to Jo'burg Monday next.

Then helicopter to a small landing-place 10 kilometres due north of Marula Grove. *If any police or army personnel accompany Yates, the hostage will be killed immediately*. The pilot is to remain with the chopper. At midnite Yates must walk *alone* 5 kilometres north-east of the landing site towards the river, where he will see a solitary hollow baobab tree. In this hollow he must place one (1) million used rands, large denominations. If the South African or British Governments refuse payment the family of the hostage must raise the money. There will be no bargaining. Yates will be given full instructions for the release of the hostage as soon as the ransom has been counted. If these instructions are not followed exactly, the hostage will be killed. Signed: Maud Carpenter.

Her father heaved a heavy sigh. 'Go on, Jane. There's a postscript. I attach great importance to it. Read it aloud.'

'It seems to be directed at you personally, Daddy. Gran says: "I am unharmed so far. I count on you, Hugh Etheridge, to obey my instructions faithfully, whatever the cost to me or mine. Maud'."

'Well?' He was watching his daughter intently.

She was frowning, re-reading the letter and the postscript carefully.

'I don't understand its purpose. It's just a re-iteration of the ransom demand and instructions . . . Ah, "*instructions*"! There *is* a message for you personally, Daddy – something she doesn't want the kidnappers to spot!'

'What makes you say that?'

'Why should she say "obey *my* instructions faithfully" instead of simply "obey instructions"?'

'We'll consider that point later. It was clever of you to spot it. Meanwhile, anything else strike you?'

'The kidnappers don't announce themselves. I thought that was part of the game these days. A sort of preliminary to haggling and a political justification for the crime.'

'That's what occurred to me. This doesn't appear to be a political or liberation group crime. They're not asking for arms, or exchange of prisoners anywhere, as part of the deal.'

'Mmm . . . and why should the kidnappers stipulate Yates by name? Of course they obviously know the Embassy set-up and Gran's relationship to it, but why specify Desmond?'

'Perhaps it was your grandmother's wish – and her way of telling us that she has a certain standing – even influence – with her captors. She's persuaded them that Yates is a trusted junior, the best choice for an important confidential – possibly dangerous – assignment. Carrying a million rands in cash anywhere is putting one's life on the line.'

'That makes sense,' agreed Jane. Her eyes and lips had softened, for she felt that her grandmother was saying, in effect: 'Let your young man handle the tough side of the action, Janie. I have faith in him.' She was proud, but afraid for Desmond. She raised her head and faced her father. 'That p.s. to you, Daddy. It seems to me that Gran's asking you to convince the family that, if necessary, it's up to all of us, collectively, to find some way of raising the ransom – though she must know it can't be done in one whack. Her personal instructions are that we must be prepared to cripple ourselves financially, if necessary. Her words are ". . . whatever the cost to me or mine".'

'So that's the interpretation you put on them?'

'There can be no other.' She hesitated and looked up at him. 'Or can there?'

He drew his daughter to her feet and took the ransom demand from her. She shivered at the cold touch of his hands. His fine-featured face was grey and drawn.

'She trusts you, Daddy. She's put the full responsibility squarely on your shoulders. You must do as she wants – at any price.'

'Jane,' he said. 'You don't know what you may be asking of me. Think well about her conversation with Kim Farrar at Johannesburg Airport and then analyse this postscript again. In the morning we'll discuss it thoroughly. Kim and Desmond each have one of these photostats. Go to bed now. We'll all think more clearly about this business when we've slept on it.'

Jane, who normally woke at seven-thirty when the African maid, Salima, brought her morning tea, found herself wide awake listening to the chorus of birds in the trees and creepers as the rising sun gilded the Cape Flats and the shreds of fleeting cloud against the pure blue of the early morning sky.

Her windows and curtains were wide open and the swimming-pool beckoned. Someone was there already. She recognised Kim and thought: Lucky chap, he's swimming in the raw. Daddy won't let me do that because of the gardener and Elias.

Poor Elias! Suddenly the events of the night and the past month blazed back into her consciousness with sickening impact. She must go down and talk to Kim. And soon Des would join them. His tiny flat was near the Embassy and it was his habit to take a morning dip in the pool before going to the Chancery in Cape Town.

She slid her copy of the ransom demand into the pocket of her floral towelling wrap, before running downstairs and across the lawn.

Kim sat on the edge of the pool, a towel round his waist, and watched her approach. Graceful as a young animal, he thought. There was colour in her cheeks and her eyes glowed as she greeted him, flung off her wrap and plunged into the water, doing half a dozen lengths with a fast powerful crawl. As she climbed out and joined him, her dark mane clung to her face and shoulders. She shook her head free of the wet strands and ran her fingers through her hair.

'You looked splendid sprinting across the lawn,' he said. 'What's more, you swim very well.'

She laughed. 'I'd rather swim in the sea than in fresh water, though. Wouldn't you?'

'Equatorial seas aren't bracing. I'm longing to try the Cape surf.'

She looked up suddenly towards the house.

'Here come Daddy and Des.'

Farrar rose. How spare he was, feline in movement, lazy, supple and watchful. Did he have a home some place? He didn't look married, but who could tell?

After their dip the four of them sat on the poolside.

'Now,' said Sir Hugh. 'We've all had a chance to think about that ransom note. Kim, I'd like your view first. You're outside the problem so perhaps you can see it more objectively than we can. The postscript, of course, is extremely significant.'

Yates was watching Farrar's face intently. He saw the dark brows knit.

'It can be read two ways,' Farrar said at length. 'A command to do all you can to pay the ransom, even if it means depriving Mrs Carpenter and her heirs financially.' He hesitated. 'Or, I suppose, it could be quite the contrary.'

'Which way do you take it?'

'After that curious conversation with Mrs Carpenter at Johannesburg Airport – and the way she hammered out her theories – I'd be inclined to think she is telling you, sir, that she's prepared to stake her life to prove her point. The ransom demand should be refused.'

'That's too extreme!' Desmond exclaimed. 'No one would accept the possibility of being murdered without a fight – least of all Mrs Carpenter. She enjoys life far too much.'

Sir Hugh's eyes rested on his daughter's face. 'What do you say, Janie?'

'I think I agree with Kim,' she answered slowly. 'But I need actual proof that Gran has bound you down in some way, Daddy. It's not enough that we all know her views. She often throws out controversial ideas just to start an argument. Putting them into practice is another matter.'

'Testing her theory to her own destruction?' He frowned. 'That's exactly what I have her written orders to do. The document is locked in my safe. You shall see it later. It's my conviction the postscript to the ransom note is insisting that I respect what she calls her Creed and obey *her* instructions –'

Jane cut in without a moment's hesitation. 'If that's so, Daddy, your duty is to disregard that Creed. Refuse to be bound by it! People believe themselves capable of sticking to their principles, but they could change their minds under pressure. We must do everything we can to raise that money. Gran's not expendable! If necessary we must play for time.'

'I'm going to telephone London this morning. After we've conferred I'll tackle the Government of the Republic – the P.M. if necessary. If one or both fail us, we have to set about breaking family trusts. It won't be easy. It could take weeks.'

Jane slipped on her loose wrap.

'That Creed, Daddy. I want it now.'

'Very well,' he said. 'You won't like it. But it's your right to see it. Your grandmother wants it published *in toto* if . . . anything happens to her.'

3
'The Carpenter Creed...I know it by heart.'

Lady Etheridge had a luncheon engagement, so Jane was alone in Sir Hugh's study when the telephone rang just after noon. She loved the bright little room which smelt of leather, polish and books, and when her father was at the Chancery in Cape Town she often used his big mahogany desk for her own correspondence. She took up the receiver and heard Farrar's deep voice – a good radio and T.V. voice, she thought – 'Jane? Listen, things are sticky this end. If I come back to the Embassy now, could you give me an hour or so –'

'Of course. And a bite – cold meat, salad, cheese.'

'Perfect.'

Within twenty minutes she heard him park his hire-car in the drive and ran to meet him.

'I'm so glad you've come! Just wondering what's happening was getting me down.'

'Me too. Where can we talk and not be interrupted?'

'Daddy's study. D'you want a drink?'

'No thanks.' Crows' feet crinkled the outer corners of his eyes. 'Not just yet.'

It was cool in the study and the scent of honeysuckle came through the open window with the shrill voices of a pair of tiny jewel-bright sunbirds hovering over the creeper.

'What news can you give me?' asked Jane.

'H.E. spent an hour conferring with London this morning. No

dice. H.M.'s Government reckons Mrs Carpenter's disappearance is bound to be bad for South Africa's tourist trade and it's up to the Republic to take full responsibility and produce both the ransom and your grandmother. So your father's seeing various ministers – and possibly the P.M. – this afternoon. Then he'll report back to the Foreign Office. After that he'll give out whatever information is for general release. I'm to be at the Chancery from three o'clock onwards.'

Jane, who was sitting on the swivel chair at the Ambassador's desk, whirled round and sprang to her feet, facing Farrar.

'So the buck begins to be passed to and fro! And, in the meantime, we don't even know where Gran is – or who's got her – and the hands of the South African police and border-patrols are tied by the threat in the ransom note. If we're forced to raise the whole million rands privately, as a family, it'll take time. What's to be done?'

'That's what I want to discuss with you. Action. For a start, what about that Creed of Mrs Carpenter's? I'd like the victim's views in black and white, as opposed to a casual conversation between strangers. Your father hasn't taken me into his confidence about the Creed yet – he's hardly had time – but he did mention that you had a copy.'

'I have. And you must see it. We need all the brains and help we can get to unravel this mess.'

She turned to the desk again and handed him the xeroxed copy. 'Study it carefully, Kim. Though some of it's irrelevant to the present situation, it's all very characteristic of my grandmother, as Mabel points out.'

'It's very important to know how Mrs Carpenter's mind works – and to gauge the strength of her resolutions, relevant or not.'

'I'll leave you while I see Salima about our lunch. Poor Elias will be out of action for the next few days. He's doing well physically,

Dr Grobbelaar says, but his brain, it seems, is a race-track with the spotlight on a black electric hare pursued by a leopard and an Alsatian! We'll eat here in the study. I'll make sure we aren't disturbed. Does Daddy know where he can find you?'

'Yes. In fact, it was his suggestion that I come back here and talk things over with you.'

When she rejoined him, he said, 'I'd like to take this with me and get Desmond to xerox it for me.'

'You'll need Daddy's permission. It's his property – for the present.'

He shifted his ground. He wanted very much to know what every clause meant to Mrs Carpenter's grand-daughter – exactly where *she* placed the emphasis. As Desmond had told him, they were very close – and very alike.

'Will you read it aloud?'

She hesitated as she took the pages from him. He pleaded.

'Please, Jane. It's important to study this together.'

Farrar relaxed in her father's leather armchair while she stood beside him, leaning against the wide desk, as she read slowly and carefully. If she was conscious of his intent dark eyes on her face and hands she gave no sign.

'"To my son-in-law, Sir Hugh Etheridge, British Ambassador to the Republic of South Africa.

'"In the sixty-two years since my birth the world has changed beyond belief. The scientist – Godlike or diabolical – is now the universal master. His discoveries have made us almost shock-proof. But not quite. We still shudder at deliberate cruelty inflicted upon the innocents among us – children, animals and the totally defenceless. Yet, in most civilised countries, even those who corrupt, torture and murder for kicks need no longer fear the death sentence. Instead, they are accommodated, guarded and nourished at the expense of impoverished and over-crowded

States, as are the living dead (deprived, by accident or senility, of thought and function), the criminally insane and the congenitally handicapped beyond hope of normal growth or existence.

'"The time has come for stocktaking. This I am trying to do, reducing countless general principles to a few simple pointers on the road towards sensible population control and stringent discouragement of violence. Somewhere along this track there may well be a signpost especially for me! I hope that I shall have the sense to see it when I meet it, and the will and courage to heed it."'

Jane drew a long deep breath.

'The letter is signed by my grandmother.'

She turned to the door in answer to a light tap and called 'Come in!' Salima, plump and doe-eyed, wheeled in the luncheon trolley and hesitated with a smile.

'Is it all right, Miss Jane?'

'It's fine. Just leave it and I'll ring when we're ready for you to bring coffee and fetch the trolley.'

Farrar filled two wine-glasses from a carafe of iced white wine. He offered one to Jane.

'Let's eat later,' he said. 'This wine has a delicious bouquet – muscatel, the grapes of the sunny Paarl vineyards.'

She nodded, but she put the glass down on the desk untouched as she handed him the document.

'The Carpenter Creed,' she said, her voice taut. 'Please read it for yourself, Kim. I know it by heart.'

He took it from her. She watched him standing by the open window, the light on the papers in his hand and on the glass of pale amber wine he had placed on the sill.

THE CREED OF MAUD CARPENTER

I believe that if the human race is to survive, the problem of overpopulation, with its inevitable pollution of our planet, must be ruthlessly contained at every reasonable point in the course of a rational lifetime. At present the problem is tackled almost entirely at its source (birth control) and even there inconsistently, since a barren woman may be given her 'right to motherhood' through the medium of drugs, surgery or anonymous insemination. From the moment of birth science sustains and extends life, often beyond reasonable good sense, until a giant mushroom of helpless dependants and aged relatives weighs intolerably upon the young vital stalk of normal society, fostering resentment which erupts increasingly in aggression. Violence is in the very air we breathe. Wife and baby battering are growing crimes. Therefore elementary controls should be applied with fearless determination.

1. Where gross congenital disease is known to be hereditary in a family, that line should be terminated. (By contraceptive measures, abortion or sterilisation.)

2. If an infant should be born so tragically malformed as to be beyond any hope of normal existence, it should not be compelled to draw its first breath. (The use of passive, or, if necessary, active euthanasia in the interests of mercy and of humanity.)

3. 'Human vegetables', kept alive indefinitely by artificial means, should be permitted to die naturally and peacefully. Terminal suffering should never be allowed to continue. (Passive or active euthanasia.)

4. Political crimes, such as hi-jacking, and the murder or kidnapping of victims totally unconnected with the 'cause' should not be tolerated by the governments of the world. If they continue, a reign of universal terror will prevail. (Israel has set brave examples.)

5. Kidnapping for monetary gain can only be discouraged by the refusal of those blackmailed to pay ransom to the

blackmailers. In certain cases, if the hostage considers him or herself to be expendable, he or she should exercise the right to refuse to be used as an object of extortion.

(Signed) Maud Carpenter.

Farrar folded the sheets of paper and gave them back to Jane, his face grave.

Mrs Carpenter squatted on a cowhide mat in the sunny mountain air outside the U-shaped door of her thatched hut. In an hour or so it would be icy cold. Then she would wrap herself in her warm woollen blanket with its jet-plane design. It was a very good blanket, warm and light, fashioned in some English Midlands factory – a fitting gift from a very modern king to a respected guest.

Fowls scratched and pecked about inside the wide semi-circle of round thatched huts in company with a tethered goat whose golden eyes mocked her, as if to say, 'I too am a prisoner.' A cat with lynx-like ears purred against her bare legs and occasionally licked them with a sandpaper tongue while an unidentifiable dog shoved his head under her hand requesting her to nip off the ticks that clung about his eyes. Nearby, his mate suckled her puppies with the same indifference as the woman who was casually offering her breast to a toddler outside a nearby hut. Unless her milk dried up, she dared not wean the child without her absent husband's consent. Thus he could be sure of her fidelity. His own she did not expect. A woman could remain faithful with less effort than her husband – months, if necessary – whereas it was accepted that a healthy man could not easily be continent for longer than a week. Even so, the wives suffered cruel pangs of jealousy which sometimes exploded into crime.

At this season, the small upland kraal was a world of women, children and old folk, for the young men had gone to the towns or the mines to earn money for their families. The children attended a small mission school near the Indian trading-post about an hour's ride away, but it was generally accepted that the boys played truant in turns to herd the precious cattle. All were under the age of puberty.

In the ploughing and hut-building season it would be different. There would be joyful reunions, dancing and combined village work and play. The seeds of new life would be sown.

This hour between sunset and dusk was Mrs Carpenter's favourite time of day. Already she could hear the shrill voices of boys, between seven and eight years old, calling their beasts home by name from the communal grazing-grounds on the hillside and soon the air would be melodious with the lowing of the herd being coralled into the heart of the kraal, the byre in its strong stockade safe from the leopards and the lynx and other marauders of the night.

Outside a hut across the clearing Mrs Carpenter could see the massive shape of the King's aunt, who was also the official Rain-Maker, moving about in her cowhide toga, her hair bleached ochre-red by cow's urine and trained into a sort of busby, the traditional hairstyle of the matron. Sometimes she prepared a brew in her iron three-legged cook-pot outside her hut, singing to herself as she stirred her weird ingredients. The song sounded like an incantation, interrupted now and again as she took a pinch of snuff, sneezed loudly and spat. This musical cooking always made Mrs Carpenter uneasy. She fancied that the Rain-Maker resented her presence, perhaps because the King, on his visits, made it clear that his reluctant guest should be treated with respect. Never, in this isolated area, had anyone except her colleague, Doctor Samuel Santekul – the Witch-doctor from the Big River – challenged her authority, and that was natural enough, for Santekul was acknowledged to be the most powerful sorcerer in Nyangreela. Also, his fees were the most exorbitant, so he was much respected for his wealth and wisdom and the quality of his flocks and herds.

When night fell the pot on its tripod would be carried into the Rain-Maker's hut to simmer over the central fire of sticks and dried cowdung.

Really, thought Mrs Carpenter, sharing this primitive village life in the continent of my birth is a unique experience. I wonder if it's basically so very different from that of the remote English hamlets I've chosen as the settings for my favourite thrillers? I've cooked up some pretty fearsome mixtures in my own literary stew-pot – local superstitions and hauntings, the evil eye, wicked squires, fake parsons, half-witted yokels and all the local gossip that makes rural life so intimately intriguing in a little place where everybody is concerned with everybody else's business. After all, people are just people, wherever they happen to be. These are only unusual because they are all, in some way, personally connected with the King. This is his own mountain spa.

I'd like to know what that aunt of his makes – or will make – of me? She gave a small shudder and wondered, as she often did, just how long she had been a captive here. Certainly three weeks. Perhaps longer. She could remember Marula Grove and going to the loo by the thorn fence with a torch. It had been a moonless night. Somewhere an animal had grunted and, as she'd stepped out of the little wooden 'sentry-box', she had been aware of some creature in the shadows. It had pounced on her before she could cry out. She'd felt a strange-smelling pad cover her mouth and nose. She shook her head at this point in her attempt to re-create the attack. Everything thereafter was blank until she'd woken in this hut to see the elephantine form of the Rain-Maker looming over her, the monstrous moon-face malign, yet well satisfied. She'd closed her eyes against the picture and the group of curious brown spectators in various stages of undress. Her head had throbbed horribly and her throat was dry. A boy had brought water in a clay mug and a girl had put it gently to her parched lips. She vaguely recalled a dog and the way in which the boy had suddenly played a few notes on a tin trumpet. They had sounded as commanding as the reveille, yet she had fallen back into oblivion.

Next day, when she had asked for her clothes the girl who had quenched her thirst shook her head.

'I am sorry. Those things are torn and finished. But these are okay. See?'

So Mrs Carpenter had assumed her fancy costume, an elaborate deep bead bib more beautifully fashioned and gaily designed than Joseph's coat of many colours. It fastened at the back of her neck, partly covered her naked shoulders and comfortably concealed her nipples. Her own heavy fair hair, streaked with silver, hung in a curtain to her waist. The Godiva-touch, she'd thought with wry amusement. The girl, whose name was Dawn, had stroked it in timid appreciation of its texture. She had given Mrs Carpenter a small though adequate apron to match her bib, and a pair of cowhide sandals. The outfit included a cowhide mantle and the splendid soft warm jet blanket.

'What does this pattern mean?' Mrs Carpenter had asked, touching the elaborate bib. 'I know your beadwork often signifies a message. This is most beautifully made.' Her head had ceased to throb and her interest in her improbable surroundings and situation was asserting itself.

The girl's slow smile broke. Beads were woven into the fringe on her forehead beneath a beaded band to denote her single status. She wore necklaces, copper bangles, anklets and a tiny apron but her firm india-rubber breasts and buttocks were bare as was usual with young virgins.

'I made it,' she said in her lilting voice with its precise accent. 'It means Welcome.'

Mrs Carpenter raised her eyebrows. 'So I was expected?'

She wondered wryly what design would indicate Farewell.

The girl shook her head. 'It was not made for you alone. But when you came here I added certain beads. Now it is yours.'

It was then that the King's youngest and favourite wife, Dawn's sister, had entered the hut to inspect the honoured captive.

Although she was respectfully known as 'the Little Queen' because of her youth, she was tall and handsome with a haughty bearing and manner. She carried a flat basket containing soap, tissues, toothpaste, brush and comb, talcum powder, and a flannel and a towel and offered them to Mrs Carpenter.

'I hope these will do. There is not much we can get from the Indian trader. This place is far from anywhere. Really quite . . .' She hesitated, seeking a word. Mrs Carpenter supplied it.

'Inaccessible, I understand. Thank you for your thoughtfulness.' She accepted the basket and its contents. 'Even an emery-board and a handmirror!'

She brushed her hair vigorously while the sisters watched, admiring the length and luxuriance of this light mane so different from their own.

'Where is your son?' she asked the Little Queen suddenly.

'Solinje? He is with the other boys, herding the cattle. But how can you know Solinje, my son?'

'When I woke in this hut . . . after the bad-dream . . . there were many people round me. The child was beside you. Dawn called to him to fetch water and he brought it and watched her while she helped me sip from the clay cup.'

'You remember all that?'

'That – and much more. But Solinje is not a boy anyone could forget.'

The two young women had looked from her to one another, deeply impressed. Their soft full lips had formed the letter 'O' and they had breathed out long-drawn exhalations of surprise and pleasure. 'Oohoohooh!'

For the first few days after her arrival most of the women had been shy of Mrs Carpenter, but the children had been more venturesome, clustering round her, remarking upon the pallor of her skin. Was she painted all over with ghostly white mud like newly circumcised youths, who, after the period of healing, rushed down to the river to wash themselves black once more, burning their temporary huts and possessions behind them, thereby setting aside childish things for ever in an act of symbolism?

When the children gathered to stare and chatter among themselves, putting out little tentative hands to touch her – half cheeky and altogether inquisitive – she had laughed and encouraged them, while realising that she must indeed be concealed in an extremely remote area with few White contacts. They giggled immoderately, palms over their mouths, as she imitated the clicks and tonal variations of their language in exchange for English phrases which they recited with pride when the King came to visit his 'Little Queen'.

The King's name was Solomon and he lived up to it, for he was a man of foresight and potency, and in young manhood had proved himself a brave warrior, fighting for England far across the sea in World War Two, and afterwards he had studied at Cambridge.

Solomon had many wives and families throughout Nyangreela, which ensured not only the continuity of his dynasty, but a built-in royal espionage network. From infancy his descendants learned to keep their eyes and ears open for any hint of treason. Of course there were family jealousies and intrigues but the King knew by long experience how best to handle those.

At the time of the emergence of his small beautiful country

from British protection into the jungle of the Third World over a decade ago, Solomon, then in his forties, had been Paramount Chief of his nation and at the height of his popularity. The step to declaring Nyangreela a kingdom had been simple. He had wasted no time but held a great meeting of all the lesser chiefs and headmen and the folk of their areas and explained that democracy was not a suitable form of government for an African State like Nyangreela, and he therefore proclaimed himself Absolute Monarch as from this hour. He would rule by Royal Decree and his subjects would respect the Divine Right of Kings. As the people of Nyangreela were all of the same tribe, his proclamation was received with joyous confidence and there was whistling, drumming, feasting and dancing throughout the land.

But, during the past ten years, a new spirit had begun to weaken traditional loyalties. Power-hunger stirred among his younger subjects, restlessly poised between the long past and the immediate inflammable future. They were becoming increasingly impatient for the King to assert his right, proclaim his heir and teach the future ruler how to guide the nation through this stormy era in which the mighty world powers of East and West sought to manipulate the developing African nations to their own best advantage.

King Solomon was well aware of his dynastic obligation, but far from certain whether he could impose the heir of his choice on the people in their present frame of mind. In a polygamous state like Nyangreela there were many claimants to the throne and some showed signs of forming parties. When he had said as much to the mother of Solinje she had flared up. She was ambitious for her son – her only child.

'Anyone can see that Solinje is a natural leader! Just as the missionaries tell us that when the Christ-child lay in a manger, shepherds, kings, wise men and even animals bowed down before him, recognising at once that he was born to be a king.'

'And look where that landed the unfortunate infant!' snorted King Solomon who, like his father and grandfather before him, had always tolerated medical and teaching missions of all denominations in Nyangreela. They were useful, but sometimes he suspected that they encouraged a growing tendency among the women to clamour for monogamy. One wife? Intolerable notion!

'If Solinje is to be accepted as the future king, I must remain in full control until he has proved his manhood with his courage in the circumcision rites and later with the pummelling of the bull. He is now only just seven!'

'And you are in your fifties – powerful and vigorous. Well-loved. No one will put a bad spell upon you or the boy.'

He had turned on her indignantly. 'It is *you* who cast bad spells and make a mockery of my manhood! You weaken my power when you take this new pill and refuse to bear me more children. The young men think I grow old and impotent.'

She had laughed softly and reassuringly. 'They know better – as you do.' She began to exert her own magic upon him to prove the truth of her words.

'You can make a baby with one of your other wives – that River-cow – while I teach our women the new freedoms. It is good that King Sol has a modern Little Queen. And it is good that Solinje is one alone. Special and unique. But we can, if you wish, pay Santekul and the Rain-Maker to strengthen both father and child. Perhaps your ancestors would want it. The old ways are powerful.'

His senses swam at the tone of her voice and the touch of her hands, but, even as they carried him away, he knew that she talked sense. The ancestral rites were still strong in the blood of his people. The Rain-Maker and Santekul would make a formidable combination. No one would dare question their power.

So, when next King Solomon went to the Big River, he had two objects in mind. To 'make a baby with that River-cow', and to consult Samuel Santekul, the River Witch-doctor, a gaunt attenuated figure whose dark scarred facial skin seemed sucked in upon his bones.

'What you ask will cost a fortune,' Santekul said solemnly. 'But fate has brought you here today, King Sol.'

With which he showed the King a week-old Johannesburg newspaper announcing that 'the famous thriller-writer, Maud Carpenter, will shortly be visiting the Marula Grove Game Sanctuary'. The reporter had stressed the fame and riches of this writer.

'But I know her!' gasped King Solomon.

'Do you like her?'

King Sol hesitated.

'I respect her,' he said at length. 'She is at least sixty years old and full of wisdom. The moment we met – when her husband was still alive and visiting Nyangreela shortly before independence – there was a feeling of understanding between us.'

'That is a good omen,' said Santekul. 'I will now meditate.'

And do your sums, thought the King.

So, in the end, Mrs Carpenter had been selected for high honours and brought to the remote mountain kraal.

4
'King Sol calls you "the Wise One". That's why he needs you.'

Jane's bedsitter in the Embassy was bright and airy with a glassed-in balcony and a little writing-desk in the alcove facing towards Devil's Peak. It relaxed her to watch the sunset gild the forested gorges and granite buttresses, the flight of birds across the rugged mountain-face and the ever-changing drift of clouds.

She had flown to South Africa on a three-month holiday-tour, leaving her secretarial job in charge of a friend. Her boss, an easy-going tycoon with a passion for sailing, seemed satisfied with her understudy. So long as his secretary was reasonably competent and good-looking he had no complaints.

Jane took a lazy foam-bath, slipped on a light dressing-gown and curled up on the broad cushioned window-seat. So much beauty! The garden dreaming under a rosy mackerel sky. Impossible to feel unhappy for long! Yet her eyes were sombre as they went to the photograph of her mother in a white leather frame. It smiled at her from the desk – a young woman not more than twenty-five, with a halo of fair hair, a swan neck and a firm but tender mouth.

'We were both too young when you died,' Jane whispered. 'I was only four, just old enough to recall the essence of you – laughter, gold of your hair, soft breast to cry against, my arms tight about your lovely neck, the comfort. . . . Yet under your softness there must have been a tough inflexible core, or you'd never have solved our problem the way you did. You chose to bear a child you knew should never have been born. In doing so, you bequeathed your terrible problem to that child – to me, Jane Etheridge! So what do I do?'

She started at a quick double knock on her door. She knew whose it was.

'Come in!'

Desmond Yates came in and sat on the chair at her desk, tilting it back, rocking it a little. That schoolboy habit! Jane smiled.

'You look sort of rumpled and distraught. What's going on at the Chancery? Why isn't Daddy back yet?'

'He's surrounded by his senior staff and advisers. He's dismissed the cubs – like me – and is keeping the line to Liphook, Hants, very busy indeed.'

'Liphook? That's my cousin, Pam Chalfont. You'd better tell me everything from the beginning.'

'Mind if I smoke?'

'Go ahead.'

'The beginning was London, of course. Whitehall. No dice. They passed the buck smartly. South Africa values her tourist assets. Let the Republic foot the bill! So it was the Prime Minister of the Republic next. Can you picture it, Jane?'

For a moment laughter flickered across her face. 'Daddy, suave but decisive, eyes, very steely, fixing the P.M. and trying to hold him down. The P.M. courteous and unruffled, solid as a block of wood, a man with a good case and no intention of being pushed around. Probably offering Daddy tea.'

'Cut the tea. For the rest, you're on beam. The devil of it is that the P.M. has a good case and we haven't. The points he made were valid enough. Marula Grove is not a National Park and in no way the responsibility of South African Tourism. Tourists who go to

Marula sign a form that they do so at their own risk. With which he shoved a paper across the desk, and there it was under your father's elegant nose, duly signed, of course. Then the P.M. added, "Mrs Carpenter is resident in the U.K. and holds a British passport." He offered his . . . condolences . . . and regrets.'

'Not *condolences*, Des! Gran kidnapped is nobody's baby, except her own family's.'

'Right. And the Bank of England would hardly be happy to send a million rands out of England into South Africa at the drop of a hat. Though I suppose, in the circumstances, something could be arranged.'

'What was Pam's reaction?'

'Your cousin Pam feels it was all H.E.'s fault for permitting her grandmother to "embark on such a dangerous enterprise with all Africa's borders aflame".' He stubbed out his cigarette angrily. 'Her words, not mine. They upset H.E. very much.'

'Damn! I can just hear her! "Dangerous enterprise" indeed? It shouldn't have been. Anyway I'd be sorry for anyone who tried to hold Gran back once her mind was set on *any* enterprise. Pam's a skinflint – what she has she intends to hold. What about Uncle Jim Carpenter and Co.?'

'He said he'd used most of his fortune to create . . . unbreakable trusts for his children. It would take time to raise his lot's share of a million. But he'll . . . look into it.'

'Gran only had three children – my own mother and Pam's mother, who died last year. And, of course, Uncle Jim, who'll contribute, if he can. He's a dear. But it's a question of time, isn't it?'

'I hate to say this, Janie, but hostage cases can drag on interminably. The deadline is announced and then set back again and again. The kidnappers are usually quite unpredictable. They alter their demands. They get panicky and settle for less, or get greedier if they think they're on a good wicket. We've no means of judging as we don't even know the individuals concerned.'

Jane frowned, her lips set. 'The only thing I do know for sure is that we've got to wring that ransom money out of the family somehow, each of us giving what we can afford – more than we can afford, if necessary! At least I've got the capital of my twenty-first birthday present from Daddy and everything that Mummy left me outright. I can give it all. I earn my own living, anyway. Perhaps we can borrow against our combined family securities.'

She slid from the window-sill with a sigh. 'Please go now, Des. I must get dressed.'

'We're dining in my flat – just you, Kim and me – to pool ideas and help back up whatever H.E. decides. I'll wait for you downstairs. Your father won't be home till late and he'll be very tired. The sooner Mabel turns him in and gives him a tranquilliser the better.'

He spoke with his lips against her cheek, his hands, under her bath-robe, held her to him. The straight smoothness of her back yielded as he drew her closer.

'Jane, I love you. God, how I love you!'

She raised her face to his, dark hair falling away, downcast lashes shadowing high cheekbones, full, soft lips inviting. His touch was gentle but insistent, exploring her slight body, the firm silky quality of her skin. She forced herself to draw away from him. Her voice was choked as she said: 'Go, darling, go!'

She heard the door close quietly behind him and leaned against the desk. After a moment she put out her hand and turned the photograph of her mother away so that it faced Devil's Peak, mysterious against the darkening sky.

The dinner things had been cleared from the L-shaped living-room and Desmond, Kim and Jane sat on the little stoep of his flat which led into a long-established garden where huge magnolia trees sported the last of their white waxen blooms among the broad blades of their gleaming dark leaves. Somewhere bats feasted on the fruit of a peach grove.

'Kim,' said Jane suddenly. 'Is there no chance that the popular press – some paper – might be willing to contribute to the ransom if you promise them an exclusive?'

His smile was sardonic. 'Do you think I haven't tried that? The trouble is there just isn't a story until something dramatic develops. Fleet Street is on its uppers at the moment, as you know. When we get Mrs Carpenter back she'll be able to command her own price – but . . . ?'

He shrugged his broad shoulders and the question hung in the air. When – or if . . . ?

'H.E. had a go at her publishers,' added Desmond. 'They were very upset but helpless. They're only just keeping their heads above water financially as it is – '

'Maud Carpenter does more than her share to keep them afloat!' snapped Jane, 'but I suppose one has to face the fact that, if Gran does the Indian rope trick, it's the end of a reliable annual output – "a Carpenter for Christmas".'

'Janie,' said Desmond. 'We're wasting our time on this sort of speculation. I've been watching H.E. in action today and I can promise you the financial and administrative side is best left to him. In the end Mrs Carpenter, herself, will find some method of forcing an issue. Believe me! Meanwhile Kim and I are in the action department. And I guess you'll have to be on standby, wherever and however you're most needed. H.E. is already about to lay his hands on what he calls "an adequate first instalment as a bargaining point". He'll be in a position to send me to Johannesburg on Monday's early flight, as commanded by the kidnappers, unaccompanied, except for the small fortune in my brief-case!'

'Tonight is Friday!' she exclaimed. 'There's still so much to be done. A helicopter to be chartered from Johannesburg to the 'copter-pad north of Marula Grove – '

'That's where I come in,' cut in Kim. 'I hold a pilot's licence, and the boys who own and charter the choppers in Johannesburg have helped me out on various occasions. I've booked to fly up tomorrow – Saturday a.m. – to arrange all the details. Everything for Part Two of Operation Snatch-back will be on the line when I meet Des on Monday at Jan Smuts Airport.'

Jane looked at him thoughtfully. She rose and touched Desmond's arm.

'D'you mind if one of you takes me home right now? I want to pack a few things. I can't stay down here at the Embassy out of the action. I want to go along with Kim tomorrow and be in on everything with both of you, just as far as is reasonably possible.'

Kim shot Desmond an enquiring and rather disapproving glance. Yates grinned at him.

'Take her home, Kim. I guess we all need an early night. As for the rest, Janie did say "as far as is *reasonably* possible". Shall we just let it go at that and trust to her good sense?'

Jane's dark eyes sparkled with excitement as she turned towards Kim. 'If you have dates with any of your . . . sources I won't interfere! I'll be staying at the Airport Hotel – a contact for Daddy and Des, should they need one.'

He laughed. 'Fair enough. G'night then, Des. We'll be seeing you Monday.'

Mrs Carpenter drew her blanket more closely about her as the light waned and the smoke of cooking-fires rose in an acrid blue haze to umbrella the mountain kraal against encroaching nightfall.

By now the ransom letter would have been delivered at the Embassy. Hugh Etheridge would understand her postscript. But would Jane accept it? *And had Jane found and saved that Journal of Personal Problems, written so long ago, with all its implications as cruel and clear as the Carpenter Creed*?

She did not know that sorrow had settled on her features till she felt small fingers touch her chin and raise her head gently.

'Solinje!'

'I am back with the cattle,' said the little boy. 'I bring a message.'

The smooth-haired grey mongrel, who was his inseparable companion, licked Mrs Carpenter's hand and placed a large paw on her knee. She patted him absently as she turned to his master.

'What message, Solinje?'

'My father, the King, is on his way to see us. He will visit you later, after he has eaten.'

'I am glad,' she said. 'Give King Solomon my greetings.'

He hesitated, his legs thin and shapeless as stovepipes under his short hide-mantle, open to reveal a small strawberry star on his bare bronze chest. Like a stencil, thought Mrs Carpenter every time she observed it, a birthmark that marks him as a child of destiny.

'Perhaps I will come to you with my father tonight. When you talk with him I listen and learn.'

'What do you learn? English? But you know that already.'

'Not enough. My father says English is the tongue of the Western World and the top country of that world is America.'

'Will you go to America one day?'

The boy nodded his head vigorously. 'Yes, like Dawn's boyfriend, Abelard.'

'Where did Abelard go?'

'Harvard.'

'You'll have to work hard to get into that university.'

'Yes,' he agreed. 'But Americans like Nyangreelans very much. Abelard says they prefer our Black Africans to their Black

Americans.'

'How interesting! D'you think this Abelard is a good boy-friend for your pretty aunt Dawn?'

Solinje executed a small strutting dance and blew a gay flourish on his toy trumpet, which alternated with a bamboo-pipe. The music of the pipe was sweet and plaintive and Mrs Carpenter preferred it to the trumpet.

'Abelard is big and brave and clever and my father likes him,' said Solinje. 'He is full of jokes too.'

He crouched down and peeped into her hut. 'Your fire burns low. I will make it up, and then I must go. I will see you later with my father.' He glanced up at her, his eyes respectful. 'King Sol calls you "the Wise One". That's why he needs you.'

'Well, he's certainly got me!'

Solinje did not notice the acid note in her short laugh. He darted into the hut, up-ended his leopard-skin pouch over last night's ashes in the central fireplace and stirred them with his short assegai. Soon the hut would be warm and the smoke filtering up into the thatch would fumigate any creature lurking in the plaited reeds, from a centipede to a snake. Mrs Carpenter watched the boy. When he was content that the fire was properly kindled he stood back, gratified.

'Dawn will come soon to bring you meat from my mother's cookpot,' he announced.

'Thank your mother. She is very kind. Dawn too, and also you, my Keeper-of-the-Flame.'

He repeated the words after her. 'Keeper-of-the-Flame. That is a good name!'

He saluted her gaily and ran off into the chilly dusk to greet his father.

Mrs Carpenter heard the clatter of hooves and the welcoming cries of children as they ran forward to watch King Sol dismount from his beloved palomino, the golden sure-footed mare with her flying mane, who could pick her way along mountain passes as yet unfit for the official Mercedes or any car. There was laughter and an upsurge of little waving hands cupped to catch the polythene bags of sweets thrown by the King, followed by packets of snuff to be distributed among the ancients; then the King's companion led his own horse and the palomino towards the byre, where he would groom, feed and stable them safely for the night.

It was not long before Dawn brought Mrs Carpenter a basket-work tray with her clay supper-bowl upon it. She squatted sociably by the fire as the honoured captive ate the mealie-meal spiced with chopped meat. Hedgehog possibly? One never knew, thank goodness!

'Has your boy-friend come with King Sol?' she asked Dawn, reflecting, as she did so, that it was a pity the meat was always on the high side.

The girl shook her head. 'He is young and very clever. He travels a great deal on the King's business. But soon I will be going back to Hydro-Casino where our parents live – his and mine. When he is not travelling Abelard manages the Casino.'

'When you are married will you live there?'

'Quite near. It is a good climate and there is a fine school close by. It is multi-racial, and boys and girls come there from many countries. I was educated there.'

'You are a credit to your school. When the students leave, I gather they often go to English or American universities.'

'Yes. Or sometimes to China or Russia. They see the world.'

'And learn a great deal, I've no doubt.' Mrs Carpenter spoke tersely, although her mouth was full of maize – and hedgehog?

'Oh, yes,' agreed Dawn airily. 'Some things good, some bad. Even at Hydro-Casino Abelard says a new type of girl is filling the eye.'

'What type?'

'All sorts.' Dawn giggled and covered her mouth with her hand shyly.

'Go on, tell me.'

'Well, there are . . . sorts of stage-managers . . . what do you call them?'

'Entrepreneurs?'

'Yes, that's it! They want our girls to train as entertainers for men's parties. They say the girls will be hostesses. Like Japanese geishas. You have to look nice and smile a lot and prepare food, offer wine, sing and strum a guitar – nothing else, you understand–'

'Unless you invite it – and the price is right?'

Dawn shrugged, her expression mischievous, and Mrs Carpenter persisted. 'What about Black bunny-girls? And maybe strippers?'

'Why not? It is the custom of White peoples' cabarets everywhere.'

'What does King Sol say?'

'You'd be surprised.'

'I doubt it. Try me!'

'He says the White man is as cunning as a jackal and wise as a serpent. He says last century White men from over the sea came and bartered beads, greyhounds and champagne in exchange for Nyangreelan land. Our Chiefs knew no better! But now we have the land back and also much of the White know-how for improving our crops and cattle.'

As Dawn hesitated, Mrs Carpenter laughed. 'And now no doubt the White man finances your casino and exploits the human weakness for a gamble and a girl, but this time you share the profits and keep your country! So it's fun and games all round.'

Dawn's slight frown creased her smooth forehead.

'Not quite. These . . . entre – '

'Entrepreneurs? What more can they want?'

'They want to make tourist attractions of our ritual ceremonies. Dr Santekul from the Big River foretells disaster for our people if we use our secret tribal mysteries as public show. Our ancestors have warned him.'

'And what of your modern young Abelard? Does he laugh at the predictions of the old-fashioned Witch-doctor from the Big River?'

For a moment the girl's face paled.

'Dr Santekul is a famous sorcerer. Even King Sol consults him about all matters of importance to our nation. Such a man is timeless. You must know that, Wise One. Abelard certainly does. Dr Santekul is his kinsman.'

She spoke reproachfully but with dignity.

'I see that your bowl is empty. I must go now. You will wish to prepare to receive the King.'

Never underrate the sorcerer, thought Mrs Carpenter, as the girl left with the little rush tray. He or She is Africa!

5
'For You, King Sol,...the old ways are best.'

Mrs Carpenter lit the oil lamp next to her divan bed, carefully adjusting the wick, for fire, like an ancient god, could bless or destroy, especially in a thatched hut.

The divan and two low *riempie* chairs had been ordered for her by the King. Straw-stuffed cushions with hand-woven covers hid the neat hide thongs of the wooden chairs and were scattered over the jackal kaross on the bed – civilised extra luxuries that established her prestige with the women.

She turned as she heard footsteps outside and the explosive belly-laugh of the King, combined with the eager barking of Solinje's dog, and the bamboo flute and dancing feet of the boy. A glow flowed through her veins that had nothing to do with the hut-warmer. The exuberance of King Sol's personality preceded him and fired her own flagging vitality with renewed vigour.

Solinje came first, the herald, swaggering in his best and brightest blanket and a minimal loincloth. The dog whined affectionately, licked Mrs Carpenter's bare ankles and looked up at her with melting amber orbs as he offered his paw. She shook it solemnly and then gently tapped it away as he repeated the gesture again and again like a cannine automaton.

'Dog,' she said. 'Enough is enough.'

Then the doorway darkened and the King entered.

For a moment Mrs Carpenter, taken completely aback, lost her composure. Usually he wore a suit, or a blanket or, occasionally, military uniform, but khaki, even adorned with medals and decorations, did not suit his complexion. Tonight he was dressed as the Warrior King of Nyangreela. He towered above her, tall, lean and finely-muscled, the firelight flickering on burnished copper skin as he struck an attitude for her benefit.

She recovered herself and bent her knee, touching his proffered hand. Her head was bowed, her back rigid, and, despite the fantasy of her own costume, there was real dignity in the obeisance.

'Welcome, King Sol!'

Her astonished reaction to his attire delighted him. As she drew erect he threw back his head and his resonant bellow of mirth echoed up to the dark rafter-poles.

'Well, Mrs Carpenter? You asked for it. It is less than a week ago when last I came to see you here. Yet now you scarcely recognise me.'

'You wear your regalia at my special request. I couldn't appreciate it more! But just for a second it was a shock. You whizzed me back in time more than a quarter of a century. I recognised King Sol all right, but I was looking at the young Paramount Chief summoned from studies at Cambridge to rule his people at the death of his father.'

'You and your husband were house-guests of the British Resident Commissioner here in Nyangreela. You were among those who saw my warriors dance in the great curve beneath the Horned Hills of the Ancestors.'

'Many of them, like you, had been in battle overseas. But that day, they whistled and stamped in their pride like their forefathers, they carried their *knopkieries* aloft and their shields were laced with throwing-assegais. Afterwards they sang a song so moving that it made me cry.'

'The song which lamented the death of my father. It was followed by another celebrating my inauguration as Paramount

Chief.'

'And after that there was the National Anthem to acclaim your accession. Solemn and impressive.'

King Sol nodded, stirred by memories grown dusty with time. Suddenly he clapped his hands and the boy crouching at his feet sprang to attention.

'You, Solinje, fetch a calabash of beer!'

The boy darted off to do as he was told while Mrs Carpenter frankly admired the King.

The King's loins were covered by a leopard-skin draped across a short beaded kilt and across his broad bare torso was a sash of elaborately embroidered pink beads. His anklets were white sheepskin and copper gleamed on copper arms and throat. His powerful frame seemed to Mrs Carpenter strangely at odds with the delicacy of his long hands and small close-fitting ears. His square beard jutted arrogantly from his chin, and, with every movement of his head, pink flamingo feathers, the emblem of the royal clan, quivered like darts in an astrakhan skull-cap.

Solinje brought the calabash of maize beer and a clay loving-cup which his elders shared, and into which he too dipped from time to time, squatting and listening intently as his father spoke of Nyangreelan folklore and of wild beasts and wizardry. The King's eyes narrowed when he told tales of hunting and feasting. It's like a medieval hunt in England, thought Mrs Carpenter, or even hunting today. There are patterns and laws observed by the quarry, the hunters and the surrounding populace. And after the blood-lust is assuaged there's the inevitable finale – the climax to the chase – the lust of a man for a woman and possession without tenderness.

Mrs Carpenter said: 'The day of your inauguration as Paramount Chief you told me that you intended to collect and record all the songs and music of your people. Do you remember that young warrior who sang a splendid solo?'

'Yes, but those songs are hard to pin down – like calypsos – because the young men sing any words that come into their heads, any tune – individuals boasting to make themselves brave. But the ceremonies that mark the seasons of the earth or the changing stages of human lives are beautiful.' He paused and added with a touch of melancholy, 'When the hut-making season is at hand and the young girls gather the reeds, or when the first crops are ripe, there is some wonderful dancing.'

'Such customs should be kept alive,' she said. 'Immortalised by the theatre. They are part of a cultural heritage.' She accepted a draught of the loving-cup he offered her.

He puffed at his little pipe with the filigree cap.

'I have photographed our traditional ceremonies and I have written about their origin and meaning in a notebook. Also my recipes.'

'Your recipes? Ah yes, King Sol, I remember now. You told me also that day how you hoped to get the herbalists to tell you their secrets such as the ointment that immunises a barefoot herd-boy from snake-bite, and many strange cures and love-potions – even death-spells! You said the herbalists would never give away their special cures and medicaments, except possibly to you, their Paramount Chief.'

King Sol laughed. 'All cooks and chemists – and witches and wizards – are jealous of their special tricks and powers and charge high prices for that little extra ingredient that is exclusively their own. I remember well that you were interested. Naturally, for you are a crime writer. You need to know the secret ways of life and death, the poisons of the Borgias.'

'But also the antidotes. When I see the Rain-Maker at her cook-pot I long to ask questions.'

'But you don't. Even I would not expect a recipe from the Rain-Maker!' He added quickly to his son.

'Solinje, the Wise One is thirsty!'

'You too, my father?' The boy offered the loving-cup to the King first, who took a generous swallow and wiped his whiskers as he passed the mug onto Mrs Carpenter.

'The Little Queen – Solinje's mother – brews the best maize beer in Nyangreela. We do not question *her* ingredients.'

'I drink to the Little Queen. And to her son and her son's father and all their descendants.'

Mrs Carpenter drained the mug and turned it upside down. The boy took it from her, laughing, but his father's face was grave. He touched the child's woolly head gently. 'Say goodnight to us, Solinje, and go to your mother. Tell her to expect me soon.'

The little lad, sleepy from the long day in the fresh mountain air, from the fumes of the fire and his share of the maize beer, left them obediently, followed by his dog. Mrs Carpenter watched him thoughtfully as he vanished into the night. She turned to the King.

'He is your youngest son – your Benjamin – and one day all his brothers will feel they have more right to the throne than he has. But even I who am in no way concerned in this matter can recognise the hallmark of a true leader. Africa will need great leaders in these troubled times.'

The King looked long and searchingly at Mrs Carpenter, as if he heard in her words the prophetic utterance of an oracle.

'By ancient custom I have the right to nominate my successor,' he said, at last.

'Then do so soon! Nominate Solinje to be King Sol II.' She laughed, and added: 'Le Roi Soleil, the Sun King!'

'But if I die before he is of an age to rule, his brothers could turn against him and my ghost would be a poor ally to the little King Sol – "Sun King" or not.'

Mrs Carpenter could sense his deep fear. Assassination. The invisible assassin was the shadow of every African leader in the world of today . . . and not only of leaders! she thought, with the acid little smile that twisted one corner of her mouth.

'What should I do?' he asked her suddenly.

'That is a big question, King Sol.' She thought for a while in silence. It was, in fact, a question she had already considered. He waited, impassive, his eyes averted till she spoke. At last she gave her answer.

'Educate Solinje to the duties of a ruler. Send him to your own English university and have him study the *Discourses* of Machiavelli. The history of Europe in the Middle Ages is the history of Africa today. Let him travel with three carefully selected older companions whose judgment and knowledge of foreign affairs you esteem, and whose fidelity you trust completely – three potential future regents, should you die before he is of an age to ascend the throne.'

'And when should I nominate him?'

'While you are still at the height of your own power.'

The King rose and Mrs Carpenter followed suit. He hesitated before bidding her goodnight and she put out her hands to him in a spontaneous gesture which he found endearing.

'My friend,' she said. 'You must talk to your doctor from the Big River. Dawn tells me he is the best in all Africa. He must keep you young and strong – as you are tonight – till your youngest and finest son can follow in your footsteps and lead your nation wisely in paths of peace.'

He looked down at her, his eyes narrowed. The hut was dim, for the lamp had burned low, the fire too, and smoke hung gauzily in the still air.

'So that is your advice? That I consult the sorcerer?'

'What is good for one person is not necessarily good for another. When Solinje is a man and his mind is troubled he may perhaps go to a psychiatrist in some fine clinic. For you, King Sol, my heart tells me the old ways are best.'

His hands were clammy as he pressed hers and she thought that his face had darkened in the gloom.

'Wise One, you are too honest. Sleep well this night.'

Mabel Etheridge waited while her husband locked the Jaguar meticulously. This was his private car, sprayed peacock-blue and upholstered in cream to match his racing colours. The mascot was a chromium model of his one-time Derby winner, Fleetfoot. As he turned towards her the late afternoon sun silvered his thick grey hair and etched the lines round his eyes and mouth. He's aged in this last month, she thought, and for the first time since their marriage twelve years ago, she felt concern for him. She slipped her arm through his.

'I used to love our Sunday rambles on the mountain, like this or in the woods. But we're so seldom alone together these days. There's always some emergency.'

Her glossy brown hair was drawn back from her face, still surprisingly young and fresh, and he was touched to see that her hazel eyes held anxiety on his account. Theirs had been a marriage of convenience. He had needed a mother for Jane and a hostess for his diplomatic life. A good dinner and the right atmosphere could often accomplish more than a formal conference between 'les chers collègues' so well versed in the art of verbal fencing. Mabel was enchanting at the head of his table but with Jane she was less adroit. She had no children of her own. When he had asked her to marry him, he had put a proposition before her rather than a declaration of love. She had been a wealthy young widow in her early thirties, amusing and sophisticated, and they had already discovered that they found each other as well suited physically as socially. She admired his flexibility – his dash as a sportsman and his authority in matters of diplomacy and protocol. She had wondered if he'd want children? Without a son the Etheridge line would end. There was no other boy to inherit.

'I suppose you'd want children, Hugh? A boy,' she had said, and added with a smile: 'As you know, it's late for a first baby, but if your heart is set on it – '

'It isn't.' The two words were deliberately spoken. The full stop. They took her by surprise. She felt it necessary to be perfectly honest.

'It wasn't George's fault that we were childless. I was afraid of responsibility. After his death I regretted that we had lived . . . rather futile lives. I'd kept putting it off – the tie of a child – and George, who spoilt me, let me go on leading my shallow, selfish, social existence.'

'I shall follow George's example.' Hugh's smile had great charm, and, beneath it, she sensed relief. It was the relief to which she responded.

'I suppose it's too late really. And Jane might resent it. But "The Ridge" and the baronetcy, the continuity of a way of life and tradition surely makes its own demands?'

'Not in this case, Mabel. Not as I see it. The feudal days are over. I don't fancy swarms of tourists to the Lake District, paying to stroll in my gardens and tramp through my home – or fish my reach of river, come to that.'

'You're a very private person, Hugh. Almost secretive. I think I understand.'

His basilisk stare had disconcerted her for a moment. Then he said: 'Two world wars, increasing taxation and the Welfare State have levelled off the obligations that go with an old title and a family estate. When I die the title will die with me and "The Ridge" will come into the market – like my horses. That's all there is to it.'

'Good, my darling. I'll do my best to make you happy and to

make your little daughter my friend. I just wish I had greater experience of children.'

She had never quite succeeded, but as Jane grew up, a truce between them was established and with it a certain affection took root. But Jane kept her real love for Mrs Carpenter.

The Ambassador and his wife strode briskly along the winding mountain path above Silvermine. The heather-scented air carried a tang of the sea, borne on the breeze.

'I miss Kirsty,' said Mabel. 'That little Scottie enjoyed so many things we couldn't even guess at when we took her on this walk. Her forays into the heath and the bush always amused me.'

He smiled. 'I agree. But I'm sure Elias doesn't miss Hunter on *his* doorstep.'

She laughed. 'Poor Elias! He really was terrified of that ferocious Alsatian. So were the cook and Salima and the cats – to say nothing of Sam, who was petrified. It's enough to have the police patrols going round the garden every night. Really, I suppose there's no danger till Desmond comes back on Tuesday. After that, there's bound to be another demand. Not so dramatically delivered, I hope!'

As he didn't answer, she said, after a while: 'Why did you let Jane fly to Johannesburg with Kim yesterday morning?'

'My dear girl, how could I have stopped her? She's as wilful as her grandmother. And somehow I feel she may be a help to Kim – and he to her. We need links in Johannesburg. Kim's hands aren't tied like Desmond's and he isn't emotionally involved like Jane. He's a man of ideas and determination, a good ally. And, for his own professional reasons, he's as keen to bring Maud home alive as we are. If we get her back he'll have a world-beater told from the inside, the family side.'

'Fair enough. So Desmond goes up alone with a first instalment of the ransom tomorrow, Monday, as the note demands – '

'Not quite as it demands. The kidnappers will expect the full amount. They stipulated "no bargaining". All the same, Mabel, I'm very grateful for your financial contribution. So will Jane be –'

'Don't tell Jane! I don't want her under any obligation to me. Anyway, surely we're following the usual pattern. Demands and threats from the kidnappers, then an intermediary materialises to make an offer . . . and so on.'

'I have a feeling that this particular instance is not going to follow the usual pattern. They've not asked for hardware. No guns. No release of political prisoners. Just money.'

'I hope you've forbidden Desmond to let Jane go with them to the rendezvous.'

'I've pointed out that she's likely to insist and if he and Kim are foolish enough to agree the bandits might scoop a second hostage.'

Mabel said slowly: 'Desmond's in love with Jane. He's under her thumb.'

'In love with Jane?' Sir Hugh stopped in his tracks. He rested on his shooting-stick as if contemplating a new idea. 'He's known her since she was a young teenager. They're friends, that's all. As for being under her thumb, I can assure you that young Yates has a will and mind of his own.'

'Fine. Any man who marries your daughter is going to need both.'

'Oh, really, you women! Liberated you may be, but you're always sniffing a wedding in the offing. Anyway, as far as I can gather, most young couples prefer – '

'To try it out first. Of course they do. Didn't we?'

'That was different.'

'Because I'd been married before? The good old double standard. The married woman – widow, divorcée, or grass-widow – was, is, and always will be fair game. But now she has strong competition. Seducing a girl is no longer tabu and no father asks a young man his intentions – '

'No point. He knows damn well what they are!'

'He also knows that, like as not, his daughter is the seducer! In any case unmarried mothers are perfectly acceptable these days.'

'You're tolerant and cynical, Mabel. But Jane isn't *your* daughter. Somehow with one's own. . . .'

He broke off abruptly. His wife slipped her arm through his.

'Listen, Hugh, Jane is high-spirited and no prude, but she has a proper sense of her own value. Call it self-respect. She isn't one to sleep around and make herself cheap.'

'Girls can be swept off their feet.'

'Desmond's genuinely chivalrous and you must believe me when I say he loves Jane. He wants her for his wife and the mother of his children. They have the same background – fathers who serve their country faithfully in peace and war.' She smiled at him and gave his arm a little squeeze. 'Desmond could well be the right man for Jane if he's sufficiently strong-willed. He attracts her. That's for sure.'

Sir Hugh, surprised, looked at his wife with new and searching eyes.

'Does she confide in you?'

He observed and shared the momentary shadow of regret that crossed her face.

'Not yet. But I'm not blind. She's like you, my dear. Warm and forthcoming when it suits her, and then suddenly, for some indefinable reason, she's back in her shell, not easy to winkle out.'

With one accord they began to retrace their steps to the car, over the rise and down the decline towards the road. She took advantage of his mood – troubled, inclined to appeal to her for advice, which he usually regarded as interference.

'I often think if I'd known Jane's mother I'd have found it easier to take her place.'

She didn't have to look at him. She felt the chill of his silence like the evening breeze riffling through the papery heath and the bell-grasses underfoot. She knew that once again she had trespassed into the forbidden territory he never mentioned if he could help it. He'd been Desmond's age when he'd married a young beautiful secretary attached to the Embassy in Athens. Five years later she'd died of lung cancer leaving Jane. He had locked a door on that brief marriage and Mabel had never managed to open it. She had accepted the exclusion although she had wondered about it at first. Later she had decided that evasion was second nature to Sir Hugh Etheridge, the career diplomat, just as it was to Hugh, the inhibited complex man she had married and grown to admire. Her affection for him was, in a way, maternal. With her first husband, George, she had been in love. Jealous, possessive, passionate. Had Hugh felt that way about Ann? Mabel suspected that there was a streak of masochism in his love of Ann. It wasn't easy for Hugh to give himself to a woman. His body, yes. His mind too if her brain merited the gift. But heart and soul? That would open the gates to total intimacy. Hugh would not willingly allow himself to be possessed and thus become vulnerable. Like her step-daughter, Mabel Etheridge would have given a great deal to have known Ann. Jane's only recollections were sentient, the warmth of being loved, and an awareness of some contradictory force. Ann was to both Mabel and Jane enigma.

'So yesterday and tonight our Jane and that attractive Kim Farrar set the stage for Desmond's arrival tomorrow, Monday,' she said, and added thoughtfully: 'An interesting man – Farrar.'

'Experienced and subtle. He has initiative and a knowledge of tribal Africa. Ambitious too. He's after Maud Carpenter because she interests him as a person as well as being a possible scoop. If it can be done, he'll rescue her.'

They paused to watch the sun slide over the horizon into a purple sea; then it was swallowed, its rose-gold reflection gradually fading from the mackerel clouds above the darkening water. The shadows of approaching night seeped into the Constantia valley below the surrounding mountains.

Hugh Etheridge linked his arm in his wife's. Somehow, alone up here in the sunset, he felt closer to Mabel than he had done for a very long time.

'What were you thinking then, Mabel, while you watched the birds going home to the vleis?'

'That people – most people – are, potentially, predators or victims. Like birds and beasts.'

'And predators and victims each have their followers. Scavengers wait for the predators to eat and take what's left, while anxious flocks – nature's victims – seek a leader astute enough to save them.' Sir Hugh chuckled as he added: 'And where do I come in? Predator, victim or just plain scavenger?'

She touched his cheek tenderly.

'You're neutral. An onlooker. Uninvolved whenever possible. You could sit back and allow the victim to be devoured. Or if you felt strongly enough, you would step in to save it.'

'Or send my minions, two young men and a girl, to cheat the unknown predator of his prey.'

'Just so. But it's odd, isn't it? I could never have imagined Maud Carpenter in the role of victim.'

6
'You, my dear, would be a gorgeous bonus!'

Farrar had put Saturday and Sunday to good use. The highveld was green after recent rains and summer-lightning forked down the distant skyline as he and Jane sat on the pool-patio of the Southern Sun Airport Hotel, cool and refreshed after a swim.

'I can't believe it!' she said. 'Five minutes ago the horizon was apricot pink and now the whole world is covered in purple gauze, a sort of bloom.'

'Like ripe grapes,' he grinned. 'There's no twilight in Africa. There's day and night, and a dark curtain falls between them suddenly and theatrically.'

She held her goblet of Campari to the fading light, admiring its ruby colour.

'You and your sense of theatre!' She smiled. 'But I hand it to you for the way you've got the stage set for Des when he flies in tomorrow. the 'copter booked, the pilot none other than yourself. Charts, fuel, food, and a comprehensive first-aid kit. Nothing was overlooked.'

The hot dry air two thousand metres above sea level had added to their tan. Her eyes rested on her own long brown fingers holding the stem of the glass.

'Skin colour?' she said. 'How absurd to make distinctions! You and I could pass for brown anywhere. Not Black because our features would give us away. You're aquiline – the Roman look.'

'And you could be a Romany girl. If I cross your palm with

silver, will you tell me my fortune?'

She laughed as she took his long lean hand and studied the lines and contours.

'It's a proper mess! A good strong life-line, a clear cool head, but a heart criss-crossed like Clapham Junction. No clarity or continuity – just adbrupt severed endings.'

'How about destiny? A line of fate?'

She shook her head. 'Not you. You draw your own line of fate as you go along.'

'No Romany girl would say that. A true gypsy really sees the past and the future and tells it for the price of a silver coin.'

He put a twenty-cent piece in her palm and she set it on the table between them.

'I see a pattern spread out here that's concerned with nothing but the present.'

He laughed. 'Well done. I live in the present – *now*, whenever "now" may happen to be. Don't you?'

She pondered before answering. 'No. Because I realise that the present is the child of yesterday and the parent of tomorrow.'

'That's a pompous remark for one so young. More like a Maud Carpenter quote than a Jane Etheridge philosophy.'

'Maybe it is. But we do have a duty to the future.'

'Even more so to now. Yesterday can't be changed and tomorrow may never come.' He wanted to dispel the sudden seriousness that shadowed her face.

His hand moved to cover hers, quick to seize the opportunity and change her mood. She was well aware of his desire to touch her, the urgency of his body to possess hers. She understood and responded to it as she understood hunger, and recognised it for a physical appetite that might grow fast and become imperious.

But he allowed her to withdraw her tapering fingers, his nerves registering their shape and movement. Maud Carpenter's plight was the obsessive 'now' for Jane. Other problems, even more relevant to her own future happiness, would have to wait.

'Did Desmond mind your coming here with me yesterday morning?' Kim asked suddenly, watching her thin expressive face. 'You rather threw your decision at him on Friday night. Frankly, I should have objected in his place.'

'I take quick decisions. He realises that.'

'Does he always accept them?'

'He hasn't much choice.'

'No real authority over you, Miss Etheridge?'

'I don't recognise authority very readily.' She smiled in response to the laughter-wrinkles that lengthened his narrow observant eyes.

'Is Desmond your particular boy-friend?'

Her smile broadened, warming her face with mischief. 'Boy-friend is an elastic term. I've known Des a long time – both at home, and now here in South Africa. He's been on my father's staff since he entered the Diplomatic Service when I was still in my teens. In a life of chopping and changing Daddy likes to have a nucleus of colleagues trained by him. Dependable and loyal. Des and I were thrown together inevitably.'

'Lucky Des! But now you go your own way. You dodge the glamorous social sophistication of the Diplomatic Corps and all its privileges. I wonder why?'

'I find it amusing and interesting in small doses, but I prefer to lead my own life. I have a good job in London and holidays abroad. This visit is one of them.'

'I'm surprised you didn't do that safari with Mrs Carpenter.'

'Are you, Kim? I'd have expected you, of all people, to understand that the essence of our relationship is its freedom – our lack of obligations to each other. We often like different things. Neither of us wants to be protected by the other. I'm of age and Gran's not in her dotage. She gives me advice, and I take it or I don't. But I always consider it, because she doles it out sparingly, and I respect her experience and her perception. She sees through people. After all, as a novelist her habit is studying people. When my mother died, I was only four and I lived with her till Daddy married Mabel five years later. He was *en poste* in Teheran then. Gran made it sound exciting. I know now how clever she was in handling the situation. She turned it into an adventure for me. That's her magic. Iran wasn't difficult.'

'Was Mabel . . . difficult?'

She looked at him, half amused, a little on her guard.

'You're a good journalist, aren't you, Mr Farrar? In one probe you pick on the human interest. Mabel was patient with me – I realise that now. She did her genuine best. At nine years old I gave her a rough ride. Gran steered clear. In the end, it all worked out well enough. Life was anything but humdrum. That suited me. Later, when it came to boarding-school, I had my base with my grandparents in their country home and rejoined my father and stepmother for holidays whenever possible. But Gran was my anchor.'

'The spotlight always falls on Maud Carpenter. What was your grandfather like?'

Her expression was tender and Kim found himself touched by the softening of her full lips.

'Grandfather didn't really belong to *now*. He'd inherited money and a charming old manor house in Sussex. His whole life centred on the land and the welfare of his tenants. He shot and fished but he wouldn't hunt. He hated the kill after the cruel prolonged chase. I suppose you could argue that he was inconsistent.'

'Aren't we all?'

'I guess so. He was an Edwardian at heart, I think. He loved England, the rolling green beauty of the Sussex Downs, the trees, and the people who worked on the land and made it productive.

His favourite indoor hide-out was his library – '

'Maud Carpenter books?'

She threw back her head in laughter. 'Anything but! More likely *The Discourses* of Machiavelli or *The Natural History of Selborne*. Now it's your turn. Where were you brought up?'

'Cornwall, where the smugglers and the wreckers flourished. My father was a country parson. A man of peace. He was disappointed when I showed a strong determination to climb the slippery ladder of journalism.'

'And now you're at the top?'

'There's never any top, Jane. But I find my trouble-hunting life rewarding – for a bachelor.'

'No ties, Kim?'

'Only my mother, who understands the footloose nomad she's produced. My father died some years ago and she remarried – a good guy who suits her and bores me. P'r'aps I'm difficult. Dad and I never really got on.'

'Have you never been married? No kids?'

'None of all that. I avoid intimate responsibilities, you see. Any woman who marries a roving journalist or a sailor is asking for trouble if she cares tuppence about family life. Most women like their husbands on a lead. My type shies at the shadow of the collar!'

'Like your mother, I can understand how you feel. Of all the countries you've covered, which have you enjoyed most? Not counting Africa.'

He pondered. At last he said:

'China. Anything could happen there. It's the most beautiful and exciting country I know. I wish I could show you the radiance of the young green rice rising from the flooded paddy-fields, and the long great rivers with their sampan populations, and the junks with huge patched sails and a great eye painted in the prow. Big

Brother Bear may think he has them taped, but the Chinese labour forces are deep in Africa already. They built the Dar-es-Salaam – Kinshasa railway from the Indian Ocean to the Atlantic, and branching down from the Equatorial Belt to pierce Southern Africa. It's a beautiful example of peaceful penetration.'

'You're seeing the achievement from your professional journalist's angle.'

'Could be so. I'd rather not, though! Not now. Let's throw the ball into your court. What special place would you want to explore before universal pollution catches up with it?'

She answered without hesitation.

'Greece. I was born there and I've never been back since babyhood. Somehow, Daddy was never sent back to Athens.'

He gave her a long thoughtful look. 'A good choice. I can imagine you in the wild mountains of Delphi, haunted by gods and heroes, wandering around those magnificent sacred precincts open to the sky, aromatic with the scent of thyme and sage under the hot sun, eagles wheeling overhead, and, way down in the valley, the tinkle of a goat-bell and the thin sweet music of a shepherd boy's pipe. It's where you belong. Deep down, you're a pagan.'

So was my mother, she thought. And father? I wonder?

Farrar saw her profile, classic and carven, straight nose, short full upper lip, clear-cut chin and the long lovely throat. His desire to touch and caress her assumed a new dimension with the pagan image his fancy had evoked. He knew by her expression that he had used his voice effectively. She shivered and reached for her towel-wrap. He put it round her shoulders and felt her tremble.

'Cold, Janie?'

'A bit.'

'It's like that here. The temperature drops steeply with the sun. Shall we go in?'

'Yes, let's. I'm shivery. Maybe it's just the sudden after-sunset cold. Or it could be that I'm a bit afraid of tomorrow.'

'It could well be that,' he said. And, in his own mind, he added: As for me, I'm a bit afraid of tonight, which certainly won't do!

Desmond Yates left Cape Town by the early flight on Monday morning. He wore a safari suit and a light quilted anorak in case the ensuing night should be cold. He carried only hand-baggage; a tartan grip containing a few toilet accessories and a black leather case filled with bank-notes – not enough of those, he thought ruefully as he crossed the apron and met Kim at the barrier.

'Before we go to the hotel we'll just check on the helicopter,' said Kim. 'I reckon we should take off at three o'clock and make our landing on the clearing beyond Marula Grove in full daylight. There we can twiddle our thumbs or play scrabble till you start your solitary midnight march.'

'We may have difficulty spotting the landing-place.'

'Not in that thick bush. It's as bald as mange on a dog's back. I did a recce on Saturday afternoon. It's tiny, no runway.'

'You went alone?'

'Of course. Mission top secret.'

'Not even Jane?'

'Certainly not. The operational area is not for Jane.'

When the final arrangements had been settled with the private company, whose managing director was a friend and colleague of Kim's, the two young men caught the ferry-bus from the airport to the hotel where Yates checked in for the night.

'Mr Yates will be sharing my room, Judy, and we'll let you know sometime tomorrow how long we'll be staying.'

The pretty receptionist knew Farrar well, and she smiled as she gave Desmond the duplicate key. She was used to the vagaries of passengers who changed their minds and their plans at short notice to suit themselves or the sudden alterations of flight schedules.

African air travel was erratic in days when the winds of political and military change blew gustily through a continent torn by internal friction and external pressures.

'That's quite all right, Mr Farrar. And Miss Etheridge is in your party, of course?'

'Sure. And thanks.' It was Yates who answered her as he pocketed the key and gave her the second glance her fresh blonde charm merited. She responded with her best routine receptionist smile.

'Enjoy yourselves,' she said automatically, and could have bitten off her tongue. How could they? Of course their arrival must have something to do with the Carpenter kidnapping. Farrar had hoped to use Judy as a source of information but she had been unable to offer any lines on the case. A pity. Farrar attracted her and she would willingly have helped him; moreover she was a Maud Carpenter fan. Spy thrillers left her cold. Judy liked her villain to have a real strong personal motive for his evil-doing. In Carpenter thrillers people murdered people they knew well – and that made sense. They never shot up helpless strangers.

Her glance followed the two men sauntering towards the elevators, Farrar carrying the tartan kit-bag and the young diplomat holding onto his black leather case like grim death. Could be a fortune in there! she thought. And suddenly the goose-pimples rose on her skin. The ransom? It was not a surmise she'd share with anyone. But some time she'd winkle a hint or two out of Kim. Since meeting him she'd learned to keep her eyes and ears open and hold her tongue. On his brief visits to Johannesburg they'd met often after her working hours, and she'd noticed that he jotted down observations that to her had seemed almost too trivial to mention. He was an odd elusive figure in her reasonably settled life. He came and went. He was generous and interesting, a pleasant companion, a passionate and accomplished lover, here today and gone tomorrow into the hell and heat of bush warfare. He neither offered nor expected any form of fidelity. He belonged nowhere and to no one.

Jane was waiting impatiently for Kim and Desmond in the suite she had taken. There it was at last – Desmond's double knock. She opened the door with a surge of relief.

'I thought you'd both been kidnapped too! Why so late?'

'We had to confirm the chopper and make an advance payment, cover insurance, and all the rest of it,' said Kim, while Desmond brushed her cheek with his lips. Then he took the bag from Kim and dumped it on the table by the large window which overlooked the patio and pool.

The room, air-conditioned and attractive, was dominated by a bed large enough to accommodate a family of four. Desmond stared at it with amazement.

'Emperor bed, I see!'

Jane laughed, and Desmond relaxed as she unlocked the communicating door.

'You and Kim are here,' she said. 'And so's the bar. There's an ice-bucket and gin and tonics and beer. It's past noon and we've a lot to discuss. Let's use my room for the conference. Then we can get a hot meal in the grill and have an hour's rest before we take off.'

Kim, already in the doorway and prepared to act as barman, stopped in his tracks. Desmond swung round from the window to stare at Jane.

'Did you say "before *we* take off"?'

'I did. And I meant it. So don't let's waste time with arguments. Mine's a gin and tonic, Kim.'

Desmond gripped her shoulders.

'Your father anticipated a move of this sort on your part. He gave me a message for you. If you join us in the chopper you'll be adding to *everybody's* danger.'

'I've read and re-read the ransom note. I'm neither part of an army patrol nor the South African police.'

'You're worse.'

'Impossible!'

'You're another potential hostage.'

Desmond felt her muscles tighten and saw uncertainty reflected in her eyes. She shrugged herself free of his grip and went to the window.

She was aware of Kim setting a glass on the table behind her and of the sharp click and fizz of a beer-can being opened in the next room. Then Kim and Desmond were beside her, watching her silently as her father's message made its impact. Precise as ever, he had clarified a situation which was bad enough already and could be tragically doubled by a selfish or ill-considered action on her part – one which he knew to be consistent with her temperament.

Kim handed her a gin and tonic with a slice of lemon, his face grim.

'Where's yours?' she asked.

'The pilot doesn't drink the day he flies. Mine's a tonic.'

She nodded and turned to Desmond, indicating the black leather case.

'How much money is in there?'

'A hundred thousand rands.'

'One tenth of the ransom demanded!'

'A first instalment. It's also breathing-space for Mrs Carpenter to . . . modify . . . her Creed.'

'But they may carry out their threat to – '

Kim interrupted brusquely.

'The kidnappers aren't going to pass up the probability of a million rands lightly. This is only the beginning. There's a pattern. The snatch, the demand-and-threat, the stated deadline, the first instalment and the bargaining. We've seen it a thousand times in the last decade – longer than that. It's an old Chinese custom, always effective.'

'This time there's Gran to reckon with. Most victims aren't obsessed by her rigid principles. How can I get a message to her – that she's *not* expendable? She's worth that wretched million!'

'Easy,' said Desmond. 'Add a postscript to your father's note which I have here. It explains the difficulty of producing a million rands when there's Exchange Control.'

'Please,' she said. 'Let me at least come with you as far as the 'copter landing-pad. I'll wait there with Kim while Des goes to the rendezvous of the baobab tree.'

The fierce noonday light, filtered by the green venetian blinds, was aqueous. Even Jane's warm colouring was muted and cool. Her eyes were pleading.

But Kim's voice was adamant. 'I'm sorry, Jane. It isn't on. You may be sure the landing-pad will be watched – by Leopard-Men, no doubt! I'll be in the safe seat – the pilot's. Des, as intermediary, is necessary to their plans. You, my dear, would be a gorgeous bonus! Can't you see that if we present them with a second victim on a plate they can double the ranson . . . and. . . .'

'And *what*?'

Desmond was silent. This duel was between Jane and Kim.

'Jane, I've come from the heart of Terrorist Africa. I've witnessed – and taped and photographed – the mutilation and murder of captives in the presence of their closest relatives as examples of the fate – of all who resist their demands. So, you must believe me and accept my decision, when I say that I will not have you on this mission with us. Wait for us here and keep your fingers crossed that Des gets back safe and sound.'

For an instant she turned to Desmond, acutely aware of the peril in which he would soon be placed. He moved towards her, but she shook her head.

'I'll wait here for you both. Kim's the boss in this business, Des. He knows Africa. We don't.'

'I go along with that,' said Desmond. 'Meanwhile, Janie, yours is the hard part – the waiting game.'

7
'Good luck, to you . . . You'll need it!'

Dusk on Monday night. Jane's hotel room seemed to her like a cage. Kim and Des should be at the landing-pad by now, waiting for the hour when Desmond would have to set out alone with that meagre portion of the ransom which would surely enrage the kidnappers and perhaps cost Maud Carpenter her life.

She had acquaintances in Johannesburg and Pretoria but she dared not call them up. She had telephoned her father that Phase One of the operation had been launched but had not even risked saying the chopper was actually on its way. The guarded tone of their conversation had left her depressed and more than ever alone. Sir Hugh's voice had sounded tired and impersonal. Poor Daddy! she had thought.

She looked out at the starry sky, the powerful airport lights and the come and go of the 'fireflies' zooming in to land or rising clear of the rooftops on their way to heaven-knew-where. She glanced at her travelling-clock for the hundredth time. Eight minutes past seven. She put it to her ear. It must have stopped! But no, it ticked on at its own even pace.

A firm rap-rap cut through the tiny regular heart-beat of the clock. Jane hurried across the room to open the door and saw, with astonishment, the trim figure of the receptionist Kim called Judy. She had a sling-bag over her shoulder and appeared to be off duty.

'Please come in. Is there . . . some sort of message for me, Miss – '

'Judy Long. Please just call me Judy. I'm a friend of Kim's. We both thought perhaps you'd like a change of scene this evening.' She sauntered over to the window. 'My view's even better than this. I have a little penthouse flat no distance from the airport, and, if you don't mind a simple meal, we could eat there. I make quite a reasonable Spanish omelette.'

'I'd love to accept, Judy. But. . . .' Then, as Jane hesitated, the other girl answered her unspoken misgiving with a reassuring grin.

'Don't worry. If there is a message for you tonight, it'll come through to my personal number, and ensure secrecy not possible on the hotel exchange. You see, I happen to know what's in the wind – or part of it, at any rate – but it's wiser for us not to discuss it here.'

Jane turned to Judy with relief. At last she had someone to share her anxiety. But the thought was quickly followed by an extraordinary suspicion.

Judy's grin widened. 'Oh, my dear, it's written all over your face! I believe you think I might want to kidnap you! Don't worry. I'm on the side of the angels. I'm one of Kim's sources, as journalists like to put it. Here's my reference. It's addressed to "Jane".' She fished a small sheet of Southern Sun notepaper from her handbag.

Jane took it. It was folded but not sealed and Judy obviously knew the contents.

> 2.50 p.m. Suggest you stay with Judy Long tonight. It's just possible someone may telephone you there. Judy will explain. If you hear nothing return to the hotel with Judy when she goes on duty at 9 a.m. In haste.
>
> Kim.

Jane said: 'I'll pack my night-case right away. But I wonder why Kim didn't suggest something of the sort to me before he and Des left me here at the hotel?'

'On the way home I'll explain all I can. It's only a few blocks away. What I know is very little, but I'm one of your grandmother's most devoted fans. Well, will you trust me, Jane?'

'Of course I'll trust you,' laughed Jane, as she zipped up her overnight bag. 'I'm ready.'

Suddenly her spirits soared. Just being able to talk to somebody who really seemed to care helped immeasurably.

Judy wasted no time as she drove her little car expertly through the heavy evening traffic.

'I've known Kim Farrar for three years,' she said, 'ever since he was assigned to Africa. As you know, this airport handles a continual flow of legitimate tourists, pseudo-tourists, rogues of every nationality, to say nothing of fanatic hi-jackers. We small fry, who work at Jan Smuts, soon get a rough idea of who's who and what's what. Especially if our observation is trained for any purpose.'

'Such as newsworthy material and personalities.'

'Exactly. Kim usually stops at the Airport Hotel. He took me out a few times and quite often I provided him with snippets of information that helped fill out his jigsaw news puzzles. Eventually I acquired a sort of instinct about what or who might be significant. He's used me as one of his sources ever since.'

'It must need great discrimination – to be an efficient source.'

'You get a nose for news and you widen your own contacts and become more observant. For instance, this afternoon Bill Crombie, a ranger on his way back to Marula in the Sanctuary Cessna, dropped in to see me at the hotel and left Kim's note for you. There's a police post not very far from Marula in direct contact with Johannesburg. In an emergency Bill can get there fast and telephone a message to my flat. It was fixed up on the runway! Bill is reliable and, as Mrs Carpenter disappeared from Marula, he's particularly anxious to help.'

'So I'm your guest tonight! I'm grateful. I was shattered when Kim and Des wouldn't even allow me to go and see them off.'

'Listen, Jane, you may be sure there were people at the airport who recognised Kim Farrar. And if Jane Etheridge had been with him, any newshound would have had a scoop. All this business has got to be as top-secret as we can keep it till your father gives out his official press release. Do you realise what a heavy burden must be weighing him down?'

'I got that on the 'phone this evening. His voice was exhausted.'

'A telephone voice can be very revealing. Here we are.'

Judy's flat was as charming as it was tiny and simple. It commanded a magnificent view across the highveld which was tawny and end-of-summer now, immense, and ridged with the white and amber mine dumps, and the clustered lights of the ever-growing satellite towns on the hills and in the valleys.

While Judy pottered in the kitchenette, Jane watched the usual spectacular display of horizontal lightning.

'It's glorious – and rather frightening,' she called. Then, as Judy joined her, she said: 'Surely it's dangerous? No rainstorm, just all that visible naked electric power!'

A peal of thunder shook the penthouse. 'We get used to these dry thunderstorms,' Judy said in her quick reassuring way. Then she added seriously: 'But, yes, Jane, lightning is dangerous. The elements can be killers or life-giving, depending on the season.'

She paused as another flash lit the dusk on the rim of the veld and shimmered in the living-room, followed by the inevitable rumble of thunder.

'Not long ago,' she continued, 'a dreadful thing happened. A four-year-old Black girl was struck by forked lightning and killed while she was playing with friends in the kraal. It was a big kraal in an agricultural area not very far from Pretoria. The rains were late and the crops threatened by drought. The mood of the people of the district was anxious and nervous. The rumour got about that the child's death was due to witchcraft. Some malignant human agency had directed the lightning to the body of the little girl, and the rains had stayed away.'

Jane stared at Judy, incredulous.

'A well-known and much respected Witch-doctor was consulted and paid to smell out the sorcerer. About two thousand people watched the terrifying ceremony. The Witch-doctor picked out three men as being guilty of directing the lightning at that little child at play.'

Jane found her palms tingling. 'This could happen today!'

'Yes. Those three poor devils were immediately dragged, protesting and screaming, into a thatched hut, locked in and the hut set on fire. Nobody dreamed of disputing the Witch-doctor's findings. The crowd simply watched the auto-da-fé. But somebody – a farm labourer possibly – got wind of what was happening and telephoned the nearest police post. By the time the police arrived it was all over. The smouldering remains of one hut and three unrecognisable bodies were all they found. Of course, no one knew anything. Even the informer was only an anonymous voice.'

'Was nobody punished?'

'It's difficult to interfere with primitive superstitions and customs, Jane, especially when no witness dares come forward. By their own standards, those people have done nothing wrong. They've simply eliminated three "sorcerers" who, they believed, were a danger to their children and the whole community and its livelihood. One has to understand.'

Jane said: 'There was plenty of witch-hunting in Europe a few centuries ago for no better reasons.'

Judy agreed. 'Your grandmother wrote a splendid thriller about a coven of witches in the Isle of Wight in this century! But then, of course, she was raised here, in the Eastern Province.

That's a territory full of magic – good and bad.'

'It's not enough to understand with one's mind, is it?'

'Not really. You need to be born to it. That sort of understanding is part of our spiritual heritage. It's something in our bone-marrow when we're several generations deep in this continent.'

'Does Kim understand it? He doesn't belong in Africa.'

Judy considered. 'Oddly enough I'd say that, in his case, it's possible. He's been around here for three years and seen it for himself. Nothing surprises Kim. People can commit ghastly brutalities and, while he condemns them with his educated mind, he still understands, deep down, what makes them act as they do.'

And Des, who hasn't got this sixth sense, may have to face Leopard-Men tonight! thought Jane.

Later, after supper, she said: 'I s'pose you've heard of Leopard-Men, Judy?'

'Sure. All the tribes of Southern Africa have some sort of animal totem, but Leopard-Men are common to many of them. They're symbolic of the society of fear. They are the "hit men", the killers. Why do you ask?'

Jane shuddered.

'Didn't Kim tell you about that night at the Embassy? It wasn't in the papers.'

Judy got up and took Jane's plate with the unfinished omelette.

'Don't struggle with this,' she said gently. 'You're too nervous to be hungry.'

She cleared the table and came back with black coffee.

'As a matter of fact the story *has* got around. Something so scarey invariably does, even when the press is excluded.' She glanced at her watch. 'Nine-thirty-five....'

Jane followed the other girl's eyes as they sought the telephone table.

'I doubt if we'll hear anything much before dawn tomorrow, if at all, and we must take no news as good news. Anyway, you'll be sleeping on that divan right by the telephone. So you're bound to wake if Bill Crombie calls. I usually plug the 'phone into my own room at night, but I'm sure you'd rather answer it yourself in case a message should come through.'

'You're very understanding, Judy. I'm more grateful than I can say.'

Kim spread the chart he had mapped for Desmond and they studied it together in the helicopter, as they had done many times already, picking out the landmarks they had noted from the air.

The landing-pad was a small clearing in dense bush. The night was warm and very dark.

'There, ahead of us, is the path you're to take.' Kim's pencil followed the wavering line marked in red ink. 'The vegetation thins after the first kilometre or so, and you should see the river about here.'

'I'm not worried about losing my way. That baobab tree is an immense landmark, even from the air. Pity we couldn't fly over the river – '

'And violate somebody's airspace in this trigger-happy area? That river borders on four countries north, east and west of the Republic – three of them actively engaged in guerilla warfare. Only this tiny mountainous land-locked kingdom here – Nyangreela – is honestly trying to maintain peace and stability, to become a little Switzerland in Africa, neutral at all costs.'

'Can she do it?'

'Not easily. Marxism appeals to the young and Big Brother Bear has his paw on all the neighbouring states. He arms them and his Cubans teach the youngsters to use what is known as "sophisticated weaponry". It's every boy's favourite game – to fight, to kill, to grab what belongs to somebody else at gunpoint. Young Nyangreelans are beginning to feel out of it. The only school the kids want these days is a training-camp for guerillas. It won't be simple for King Sol to safeguard his kingdom against the new Marxist policy in Africa – '

'Which is?'

'Murder the missionaries, especially teaching missionaries, Black and White, and bustle the pupils in scores or hundreds across any border into Marxist territory and then disseminate them to guerilla training-camps both in Africa and the Iron Curtain countries. It's a brilliant conception and will give Big Brother ultimate control of one vast continent of immense potential wealth and two great oceans. The kids won't know what's hit them till they're slaves!'

'Like Hitler's youth movement? Catch 'em young, then mould 'em into shape.'

'Sure. It's infectious – and effective.'

'And in which of the river-border states is Maud Carpenter most likely to be incarcerated? Nyangreela, since there's been no demand for arms in the ransom deal?'

Kim looked up from the chart with a reflective frown.

'Could be. On the other hand, these communist-inclined states are getting all the hardware they need from Russia and may want even more ready cash than the industrialised world is handing out every time they bleat for it. Or it might just be one grasping bandit looking for a little more bread to launch a take-over coup in his own country. Talking of hardware, I'm sorry you haven't a gun, Des. But at this stage the kidnappers need their intermediary. You *should* be safe. Your job is to negotiate – play for time.'

'We've been through all that.' Desmond spoke impatiently as he stubbed out his cigarette and looked at the luminous dial of his watch. 'I'd better start my stroll if I'm to be at the rendezvous by midnight.'

'I'll come with you to the beginning of the path.'

'No. I'm sticking to instructions. They were explicit. "Send Yates alone . . . the pilot is to remain with the chopper."'

'Good luck then.'

As Desmond left the chopper, black leather case in hand, Kim was well aware of eyes in the dark surrounding bush. He too would be under surveillance during the vigil to come. His hand rested on the holster of his own loaded revolver. The South African military and police border patrols had been warned off the area as instructed by the kidnappers. He and Yates were on their own. Even Marula could not help them in the event of an attack on the chopper. But Bill Crombie, the ranger in charge, would get a message to Judy's flat in an emergency. If necessary, Kim had arranged to fly right over the Sanctuary and drop a special message in a weighted white bag as they passed over the ranger's cottage. That would mean bad news of some sort.

He watched Yates stride across the clearing towards the unknown track. He moved briskly and purposefully, and he had a characteristic way of carrying his head high and his shoulders well back as if he owned all he surveyed. Kim found himself grinning wryly. 'Good luck to you,' he repeated, half aloud. 'You'll need it!'

Apart from the ransom, Desmond carried a torch, a compass and the chart Kim had mapped out. He had never been on an African safari and most of the sounds and smells of the moonless night were strange to him. Unaccountable, nameless; now near, now far, sudden and startling in the stillness. He heard grunts, hoots and rustles off the narrow wavering trail picked out by his torch, or the sudden flight of wings from a dark canopy of leaves overhead. Often, nearly underfoot, he'd hear a squeal or a chase in thick grass with a queer rank odour. As he advanced a shimmer of fast-flowing water showed every now and again and he was aware of the vegetation changing as the thirsty roots of wild figs and tall mopani trees sought the river. Once he stopped as a deep bellow rose from some hidden pool. A hippo? There'd be crocs too. And surely Kim had said this was elephant country? Did the herd sleep at night? If so, how? And lion? Possibly. He thought that some way off he could distinguish the harsh mindless laughter of a hyena, the lion's scavenger. They'd heard that 'laugh' near the chopper pad and Kim had told him what it was.

He stood quiet and alert, wondering if he had covered five kilometres yet. The baobab should be in sight of the track. He switched off his torch, feeling curiously defenceless without its beam, but his own eyes soon adapted themselves. At some distance to the east he saw the monstrous silhouette of the vast old tree, and, poised delicately above it, a thin new moon. Just beyond the baobab's bole was the river, broad and impressive.

As he listened intently to the night's non-silence he distinguished a cough somewhere near the great tree. An animal cough? Leopard? He held his breath. Of course. Someone – some *thing* – would be watching and waiting for him! The air was mild but a cold tremor ran over the surface of his skin. He was frozen where he stood, nerves tingling, heart thumping. For the first time in his adult life Desmond Yates was extremely afraid.

He was dismayed and indignant at the discovery. Excitement he had anticipated tonight, but not this chilling sensation raising the curls on the back of his neck. His pupils had become aware of the phosphorescent eyes of nocturnal wild creatures focused upon his conspicuous figure – the wrong shape, the wrong smell, the arch enemy. Man. Desmond thought he could make out dim figures in the dense shelter of the baobab. They also were two-legged.

Suddenly some instinct caused him to swing round and he saw and smelt with horror what Elias had encountered in the Embassy garden, a Leopard-Man, his face hidden by the animal mask, his loins clothed by a leopard pelt, his hands fur-gloved with shining steel claws, and his stench heavy and sickening – the tannery odour of a badly cured kaross combined with human sweat and excitement.

The Leopard-Man was not alone. They moved out of the bush to surround him – the bizarre forms of a nightmare.

The call came through to Judy's flat at about five in the morning. Jane woke instantly from a light anxiety-ridden sleep.

The voice was deep and brisk.

'Miss Judy Long?'

'No. Jane Etheridge here. I've been hoping for a message from Kim – '

'This is it,' the voice cut in. 'My name is Crombie – Bill Crombie. I'm speaking from Marula Police Post and I have to get back to the Sanctuary.'

'I understand.'

'Good. Now here's the message from your friend. I'll read it. "Tell Judy to organise a doctor *at her flat before 7 a.m.* and to confirm the booking for two seats on the Cape Town evening flight today." That's all.'

Jane repeated the message and added:

'Is that all you can tell me?'

'That's the lot. The message I've read you was dropped from the chopper in a weighted white bag as we'd arranged.'

'Thank you, Mr Crombie. I'll give Judy the instructions right away.'

'Ah, no,' he said. 'Let her sleep a while yet! She won't let you down. Don't worry too much about the doctor part. We have a lot of minor accidents here in the bush, but often an anti-tetanus injection is a good precaution.'

'I'll tell Judy that too. It may be useful for the doctor to know.'

'Sure. Best of luck to you all. We're keeping our fingers crossed here for the principal lady in the case. Goodbye, then, Miss Etheridge.'

Jane put the receiver down. At six-thirty she'd wake Judy. A doctor? Why? What had happened to Des out there in the lonely night? Why only two seats on the late Cape Town flight? And, most of all, what about Maud Carpenter?

8
'. . . *nothing is beyond belief in this Continent.*'

Jane braced herself when at last Dr Sugden came out of the bedroom where Desmond lay.

'Don't look like that!' he said, with a reassuring smile as Jane sprang to her feet, all her anxiety naked in her eyes. 'Your young man has plenty of stamina and he'll be able to fly back to Cape Town with you by this evening. Apart from a nasty scratch on his cheek, and the three long gashes on his arm, he's suffering from shock and exhaustion. But he's all cleaned and stitched up, he's had an anti-tetanus injection and is very drowsy. In fact, he's probably dozing already. Have a look!'

She opened the connecting door quietly and turned back to Dr Sugden with a smile of relief.

'He's out for the count.'

'Good. Sleep is nature's healer, you know. I found it quite difficult to think of him as a diplomat. His attitude towards his unusual and extremely daunting mission struck me as being more like that of a commando.'

Her smile widened. 'I know what you mean. He comes of a military family. He takes events and orders – no matter what – in his stride. He's . . . uncomplicated.'

'Which is a mercy in these days of youthful introspection and hang-ups. By the way, Miss Etheridge, is Kim still around?'

'No. As soon as he'd put you in the picture about Desmond's injuries, he dashed off to Pretoria in his hire car. Half my father's staff is already there, so Kim can get through to Daddy on a scrambled line and give him a full report on what's happened. But he said he'd be back before we have to get our flight to Cape Town.'

'Splendid. Now take it easy yourself, young lady! You've been – and are – under strain yourself. You've had to learn the hard way that nothing is beyond belief in this Continent.'

'Or anywhere else, for that matter, Dr Sugden. Is there a number I can call if, for any reason, I'm worried about Des?'

He gave her a number. 'This will page me, wherever I may be. But I don't think you need worry. He'll be hungry when he wakes which won't be much before lunchtime. Just feed him and then keep him quiet till you take off.'

After he had gone she rang Judy at the hotel, bearing in mind that the reception-desk line was far from private.

'The quack says that our friend did a first class first-aid job away in the bush. So your unexpected guest is now asleep in your bed, very neatly patched up.'

Judy's tinkle of laughter came over the line. 'And our friend is on his way to Pretoria, while you, I hope, will just rest. You'll find what you need for a cold lunch in the kitchen and you can heat up a tin of soup. Oh, and when you see our friend tell him I have a scrap of news for him. It could possibly be significant. That's for him to judge.'

'I will. He'll get in touch with you as soon as he's back.'

Suddenly, as she replaced the receiver, an immense weariness overcame her. She'd take another peep at Des to be sure he was all right and then she'd lie down, leaving the door ajar between the living-room and bedroom. She must be ready to answer the telephone if necessary.

She pushed Judy's door open and sat quietly on the little chintz armchair near the bed.

Desmond had not moved. He lay on his back, his left arm in a sling across his broad bare chest. His head had fallen sideways on the pillow, revealing a vicious angry-looking scratch from the outer corner of his left eye to his jawbone. It had some sort of invisible strip-dressing to cover it and she could see the stubble on his unshaven chin and upper lip. The light, subdued by a bamboo blind, added to his unfamiliar pallor.

He looks like a child now, but he's not, as I should very well know! I told the doctor he was 'uncomplicated'. He is, of course, compared with Daddy who seldom lets the mask slip. I *can't* understand why Daddy has never told me about the curse on his family. Why, in the name of heaven, did he let me find it out the way I did? If Gran hadn't been kidnapped and I hadn't saved her 'Journal of Personal Problems' before the police went through her papers, I'd still have been in ignorance. Come to that, why didn't *she* tell me? I daresay she reckoned it was Daddy's duty. He probably insisted on her leaving it to him. I'll have it out with him the moment I get a chance!

Desmond stirred and sighed, and she held her breath. But his own resumed its even rhythm and she relaxed.

'Uncomplicated?' she repeated half to herself and half to the sleeping man. 'What did I really mean by that, Des? *Normal*, perhaps? I think I know you inside out, but will you still want to marry me when you know everything? I doubt it very much. If you feel as shocked as I do myself, you'll say "no" to marriage and make do with our love affair that can only survive till someone else shows up who can fearlessly give you everything a man has a right to expect of his wife. If you were a loner, like Kim Farrar, it might be different but you're Desmond Yates, only son of conventional parents, generations deep in service traditions.'

She wanted to touch his forehead with her lips but restrained the impulse.

'Sleep on, my love,' she whispered.

Mabel Etheridge glanced at the clock over the mantelpiece in the study.

'Just after ten. Jane and Desmond should be here any time now. D'you think they'll want hot coffee?'

'All they'll really want is sleep,' said her husband. 'They'll have eaten on the plane. But coffee will keep them awake long enough for me to hear Desmond's version of what happened. Kim gave me his on the 'phone from Pretoria this morning. But I want the facts from Desmond's angle as well. He was in a poor way when he got back to the helicopter, I gather.'

'Well, the drinks trolley is here and the percolator's bubbling. Listen! There's the car.'

Elias was already at the door, taking Jane's bag.

'Leave mine,' said Desmond. 'And Joshua can wait and drive me back to my flat.'

Elias looked at the young man's arm in a sling and the clawmark on his cheek and winced. He led Joshua, the driver, into the kitchen quarters for refreshment and speculation, hoping devoutly that no one would consider it necessary to bring Hunter and his police handler back to the Embassy 'for protection'. Meanwhile Salima took Jane's overnight grip upstairs.

In the study the Ambassador had given a stiff brandy on the rocks to Desmond while Mabel poured cups of thick strong Turkish coffee for all of them. Sir Hugh always insisted that his coffee be served as it was in the Middle East, fragrant and strong. None of this instant stuff for him!

'I gathered from Kim this morning that he's coming back tomorrow,' he remarked.

'Yes, sir, by the noon flight. He has some loose ends to tie up in Johannesburg.'

Jane glanced at Desmond and wondered if Judy could be one of those 'loose ends'. Somehow, the suspicion was an irritant.

Her father grunted. 'We need him here. The media are giving us no peace.' Then he smiled. 'I gather your assignment was tough, Des, and I don't intend keeping you longer than is necessary, but I need your version of the meeting.'

'There was no moon and the track was narrow and rough,' Desmond began. 'I saw the shimmer of water and heard the river. Suddenly there it was – the baobab. Gigantic, bloated hollow trunk, livid branches, rather sparse leaves and the curious feeling that it was all *occupied* like a savage tenement housing goodness knows what – beasts, birds, reptiles, insects! I was staring at it when they surrounded me.'

'They? What or who surrounded you?'

Sir Hugh was leaning forward, his eyes focused on the young man as if he were trying to penetrate the full horror of that moment.

'Leopard-Men with masks, spiked fur gloves and leopard pelts. Half a dozen perhaps. Two of them grabbed me and a third – with bare hands – searched me. When they found I was unarmed they laughed but it wasn't like human laughter. Then one of the gloved fellows stroked my cheek. A gentle warning, no doubt.'

'So I see.'

'It wasn't bad. It didn't even need stitching.'

'Your arm did?'

'That came later. This . . . escort pushed and pulled me towards the baobab. One snatched my black leather case and ran on ahead, fast and silent. Although they walked or ran on two legs they stank like animals gorged on carrion. They weren't human. They'd passed some barrier which divides man from wild beasts. They seemed. . . .'

As he hesitated the Ambassador said:

'It's all fantastic. Use a fantastic description if it fits.'

'I will then. They were possessed. I believe that when they put on that garb they became possessed of the devil. The real leopard is predatory and cruel because that's his instinct and the way he's made. They've corrupted it into something worse. It is a horror-cult.'

'Their intention is to instil fear,' agreed the Ambassador.

'We saw Elias that night when he was given the message – and the works,' put in Lady Etheridge. 'It wasn't only the wound that pulverised him. He could see and account for that, and his people are used to fights and lacerations. It was the mumbo-jumbo that goes with it.'

'Elias and I are blood brothers from now on!' grinned Desmond.

'Go on with your story,' prompted Sir Hugh. 'The sooner you get the facts off your chest and home to bed, the better.'

Desmond continued. 'The Leader of the Leopard Clan was waiting inside the trunk of the baobab in a low easily accessible hollow about the size of a small cave. The others made signs to me to wait outside with them. I could see the Leader and his personal aide. They wore masks but their hands were bare because they'd opened the case and were crouched over it counting the ransom money onto the floor by the light of an old-fashioned lantern. When they'd finished the Leader stowed the notes back in the case, locked it and gave it to his P.A. Then he came out of his hiding-place, and we all stood to attention.'

Desmond gulped a draught of brandy. 'He was very tall and gaunt, dwarfing all his side-kickers, but the animal mask hid his features. He addressed me in precise educated English. He had the deep rumbling voice of the true African. He said in a scathing way, "What you have brought me is one-tenth of what my Master has demanded. Have the Queen of England, the President of the South African Republic and the family of Maud Carpenter so little care for her life that they throw it away by offering this wretched sum?

My Master will spit upon it!" With which he gave quite an impressive display of what his Master's reaction would be. I said that Her Majesty's Ambassador to the Republic had explained in a letter – in the case with the money – that this sum was only a first instalment. More would follow. He patted a monkey-skin pouch hanging round his neck – his loin-cloth was leopard-skin, of course – and said: "I do not read my Master's letters. He will do so himself and send a message to Cape Town in a few days' time. My Master is not a patient person." Then he turned to my strong-armed guard and said something I couldn't understand.'

Yates paused and moistened his lips with his tongue. Sweat stood on his brow.

'The Leopard-Man on my right ripped the left sleeve out of my bush-jacket with a sharp hunting-knife. Then, in a ritual sort of gesture, he slashed my arm from shoulder to elbow with one three-clawed swipe. The Leader held up his lantern and watched the blood flow. He said, "That is my signature to show your Ambassador what *I* think of his first instalment. My Master's reply will follow." I kept my head enough to ask if he could give me proof that Mrs Carpenter was alive and unharmed. His men kept me in their grip. He said firmly: "Mrs Carpenter has been well-treated and is in excellent health. But, if the full amount is not paid quickly, she will die."'

'Have you made notes of all this?' asked Sir Hugh.

'Kim did in shorthand after he'd patched me up in the 'copter. Then later this afternoon, in Judy Long's flat, he borrowed her typewriter and made a proper report.'

'Who is Judy Long?' asked Mabel.

'One of Kim's sources, absolutely trustworthy and very helpful,' put in Jane. 'I have a copy of Kim's report here, Daddy. It's for you.'

She took a long envelope from her handbag and passed it to her father.

'Judy won't talk,' she added. 'We stayed in her flat all day – and I spent the night before with her. It was her doctor who fixed Des up this morning. Judy's one of the receptionists at the hotel, but she's a listener, not a talker.'

'Ring for Elias, Mabel,' said Sir Hugh. 'These young people have had enough. What they need now is sleep. Joshua will drive Desmond home. Tomorrow we'll get Dr Grobbelaar to have a look at his arm.'

The steward caged Kim and his Black companion with breakfast trays, clipping them firmly across their laps.

'I hate this feeling,' said the young African, flashing strong white teeth at the blonde air-hostess as she poured milk on his cereal. 'I feel like that tiny tot in the comic strips – all hemmed in and very much inclined to throw my bowl on the floor.'

'Resist the inclination,' smiled the air-hostess. 'We get quite enough tiny tots throwing things, as it is.'

She passed on, friendly and pretty. Kim's eyes followed her appreciatively. 'I can't think what they see in their jobs. They must feel hemmed in themselves, yet they never forget to lay on the charm.'

'They see the world and all sorts of people. Talking of which, haven't I seen you before some place?' He had a slight American accent.

'Could be,' said Kim. 'It disfigures the box from time to time – '

'Of course! Farrar – Kim Farrar. I'm Abelard Cain from Nyangreela.'

'Then I may even have seen you at the tables there, scooping in the shekels.'

Abelard Cain had an engaging laugh. 'Roulette is one of my many besetting sins. Thank goodness our country thrives on its playgrounds! I happen to be a Director of the Hydro-Casino.'

'Your country is a little Paradise. A fun-place. Can you keep it that way, with Africa boiling up all round you like a witch's cauldron?'

'We can try, Mr Farrar. At least our people are not divided. We are one nation, all Nyangreelans, and we have a tolerant King, who is much loved by his own subjects and respected by his neighbour states. But he's in his late fifties so there's inevitably an element of student rebellion against some of his decrees. Youth always wants to revolutionise the world.'

'Within limits, that's a healthy outlook. The most united family has a certain amount of friction – jealousy here, aggression there, resentment of control. Your King Solomon is something of a legend. To my knowledge, his authority has never been seriously threatened, but even the best earthly father is not immortal.'

'Nor is the eldest son necessarily most suited to replace his father as head of the family.'

'In the days of the Turkish Sultanate before Atatürk and modern Turkey, it was usual for the heir to the throne to have all his brothers strangled the moment the Sultan was pronounced dead.'

Abelard Cain's laugh had a hollow ring to it. 'Rather drastic, wouldn't you say?'

'A fairly natural result, perhaps, of a polygamous way of life.'

'I agree with you there. Polygamy is becoming quite outmoded in our country. After all, a man shouldn't have to marry all his girl-friends!'

Kim laughed. 'Hideous thought! But these days only kings can afford unlimited matrimony.'

Cain was relieved when the air-hostess appeared with eggs and bacon. When he and Farrar had helped themselves, he changed the conversation which, he felt, was getting out of hand.

'Are you on holiday? Or on the job?' he asked.

'A bit of both. And you?'

'The same. I'll be staying with our Consul in Cape Town. There's a little business to be done and only one important chore.'

'An easy one, I hope.'

'Couldn't be easier. My people have seasonal rituals, as doubtless you know, like your harvest festivals, Easter lambs and America's Thanksgiving turkeys and so on, and in a fortnight's time we celebrate our Rain-Making ceremonies.'

'Very important. But where do you come in, Mr Cain? Have you these special talents yourself. Are you a water-diviner?'

'Heavens, no! The Rain-Maker's is a hereditary gift. Hers is an agricultural post, not the sort you'd find at Westminster, I grant you. All she has demanded of me is two litres of sea-water taken at high tide on the night of the full moon. Our country, as you know, is land-locked. Our nearest sea is the Indian Ocean but our Rain-Maker fancies a magnum of the cold Atlantic for her special rites.'

That geographical information settles it! thought Kim. Nyangreela must be the country in which Maud Carpenter is held prisoner. And I'm pretty certain that my agreeable fellow passenger, Abelard Cain, a Director of the famous gambling spa, Hydro-Casino, has a finger in the Carpenter pie. After all, Cain is only his alias for Obito – August Obito, the powerful Head of Nyangreelan Intelligence, who is also engaged to marry the sister of King Sol's favourite and youngest wife. Kim had been doing some intensive homework on Nyangreela and he had learned from Judy that it was not by chance that he was occupying the seat next to Mr Cain. Judy had given him some useful information about that flamboyant personality who was much-travelled and well-known by the staff of Jan Smuts Airport.

'Your chore is certainly no problem. The Cape Peninsula can offer you the water of both oceans, Indian or Atlantic. You have only to paddle in and collect,' he said.

'Not even that. Our Consul has already got the necessary Atlantic water bottled in a beautiful sealed jug. All I have to do is deliver it safely to the Rain-Maker some time before the next full moon. I'm merely the messenger.'

Kim looked sideways at Abelard Cain alias August Obito and hoped he was not also alias Leading-Leopard-Man. He had grown wary of Nyangreelan messengers. However, he summoned up a smile and said, 'Then you can enjoy the sea for nearly a fortnight without any responsibilities.'

'So right!' cried Abelard joyfully. 'And I love sailing and fishing. Man, I can't wait!'

The infectious holiday spirit of the young man was obviously genuine. For the moment he was not so much the Head of Nyangreelan Intelligence as an exuberant schoolboy banging his desk-lid shut before taking a vacation.

'My friend, the Second Secretary of our Embassy – Desmond Yates – is a keen sailor,' volunteered Kim. 'He has a small yacht. Maybe you'll come out with us some time. There's good fishing round the coast.'

'You're sticking your friend's neck out, Mr Farrar. I'd enjoy it no end. You can get me at the Consulate any time. Just leave a message for Abelard Cain and if I'm not there they'll find me and I'll call you right back.'

'Fine. I'll do that.'

'But you're the elusive one at the beck and call of news. Lord knows there's plenty these days and little of it good. What story are you chasing at the moment?'

Kim hesitated. Then he took a chance.

'I'm driving myself crazy trying to get leads on the Maud Carpenter kidnapping.'

Cain said seriously: 'The media is playing the Carpenter story in a very cagey way. Too few releases, would you say?'

'Or not enough hard news. The hostage is important as a human being. She's not just a symbol. She *belongs* to millions of people. Her fans wait for the annual Maud Carpenter to entertain and relax them and distract them from plain humdrum boredom. Then suddenly she vanishes! Like one of her own characters, only more so. It's not from the rectory garden she's snatched, but from a loo in the African bush! Nobody – no group – takes responsibility for the kidnapping. There's no demand for arms and weapons. Just a million rands which will take the family a considerable time to raise. She could be anywhere in Africa by now! She's my ace headache at this moment.'

'Yes,' said Cain thoughtfully. 'She certainly must be. I can imagine too that she must be quite a headache to her kidnappers. She dreams up the most ingenious plots so why not a smart escape?'

'She must be held in some very remote place. But where? That's our problem. *Where? And who?*'

'Look, Mr Farrar, from time to time I get miscellaneous bits and pieces of information. You know how it is. People gamble and drink and spill quite a lot of beans off as well as on the gaming tables. If I get a whiff of what's cooking in the Carpenter case, where can I contact you? Your news H.Q. in Johannesburg?'

'No. The British Embassy. That's in Cape Town for the present. It moves to Pretoria at the end of the parliamentary session. Soon now.'

'I won't forget.'

'Meanwhile, I'll be calling you at your Consulate for a sailing date.'

'I'll look forward to that.'

The Cape peaks rose, blue and jagged, beneath them and then the soft wine-growing Paarl Valley spread its green carpet between the mountains and the sea. The voice of the air-hostess filled the cabin with instructions and politenesses in English and Afrikaans and the wheels met the runway of D.F. Malan Airport.

9
'I have heard of your powers, Dr Santekul.'

Kim's report to the Ambassador was followed by one of those characteristic silences. Kim knew better than to break in.

At last the Ambassador said: 'So you think this Abelard Cain could be the top level agent – the bargainer on behalf of someone very high up in Nyangreela?'

'I do. According to a reliable source it was no coincidence that he came down to the Cape on my flight and found himself placed in the seat beside mine. He got into conversation quickly, very naturally and affably. He has great charm and seems to me to be a smooth operator.'

'So, in your opinion, we should follow up this lead as soon and as vigorously as possible?'

'Without doubt. If my hunch is anywhere near the mark, Abelard Cain represents the civilised aspect of the Leopard scare cult. His approach will be interesting. We could let him make the running and then put up our own terms for a settlement.'

On the following morning Abelard Cain called on the Ambassador at the Chancery as a matter of courtesy and was received with the bland friendliness Sir Hugh bestowed on all foreigners unless, for some strong reason, he found it necessary to snarl and bare his teeth.

Although the call was a polite formality he gave his visitor more of his time than the usual perfunctory fifteen minutes. Nyangreela had, before emergence, been a British dependency, and Abelard disarmingly explained his official identity within the first few minutes. Then he added:

'I'm on holiday, your Excellency. That's one reason why I prefer to use the name which people associate with my Nyangreelan front as the principal director of the Hydro-Casino.'

'A very profitable front! I know your Hydro-Casino is a lively tourist attraction for all ages and nationalities. Farrar tells me it combines extreme sophistication with homely facilities, such as baby-sitters. Your *alter ego,* Mr August Obito, Chief of Nyangreelan Intelligence, must find it a most relaxing resort.'

Abelard's fine teeth flashed. 'It is indeed. I'd be delighted if you and your family would be my guests there some time, Excellency.'

'That would be very nice. Just at present, for our part, we are not entertaining, as our Embassy here is on the point of its annual transference to Pretoria for the winter. A proportion of the Diplomatic Corps has already moved. Added to this, we are, as you must realise, going through an agonising family trauma. My daughter, Jane, has taken the kidnapping of her grandmother very hard indeed, and the responsibility on my shoulders is a heavy one.'

'I can well understand that, sir. It was – and is – a shocking affair –'

'Which could still end in tragedy.'

'Unfortunately there have been remarkably few news items about the Carpenter kidnapping since the original story broke with its consequent stir.' Abelard's features had settled into an expressionless mould which the Ambassador decided to shatter.

'Bearing in mind your most important identity, Mr Cain, or should I, in this instance, say Mr Obito? I feel sure that you must have heard rumours, if not hard facts, about the bizarre circumstances surrounding Mrs Carpenter's disappearance; and, nearly a month later, the vicious mauling of our Xhosa butler, Elias, when a ransom note was delivered in the grounds of the Embassy. Then recently, a very similar type of mauling was inflicted upon my Second Secretary, Desmond Yates. To be exact, it happened in the small hours of Tuesday morning when he delivered a first instalment of the million rands ransom demand.'

'There have been rumours, naturally,' agreed Abelard, 'but since Nyangreela is in no way involved, my agents have not interfered with what appears to be a non-political crime committed, possibly, in some neighbouring state. Or even within the boundaries of the Republic.'

'Aren't you taking a good deal for granted, Mr Cain?'

Abelard leaned forward. 'The second short news release made only three points. The kidnappers have *not* announced themselves and claimed responsibility, as is usual in political crimes of this sort. Neither have they demanded weapons, nor even the release and return of any political prisoners held in the Republic or in the United Kingdom. One has, therefore, to assume that the whole operation has been instigated by private enterprise.'

Sir Hugh favoured the Nyangreelan with a wan smile.

'Logical enough. The Marxist stamp doesn't appear evident, but one can never be quite sure of anything. And since, happily, private enterprise does still thrive in Nyangreela, one cannot entirely eliminate the possibility that Mrs Carpenter may be held in some remote area of your beautiful country. The motive of greed is, unfortunately, universal.'

The Ambassador rose. Abelard took the hint and followed suit. His distinguished host had, as yet, the right to the last word.

'It was kind of you to give me so much of your time, sir – and your confidence.'

'It was a pleasure. As I told you, our household is in some confusion, but I hope you'll dine with us informally *en famille* before you return to Hydro-Casino or wherever else your presence may be required. Farrar or Yates will get in touch with you later today.'

When Abelard had taken his leave the Ambassador rang for Kim who was waiting in the Chancery.

'Well, sir,' said Kim. 'What do you make of him?'

'He's in it up to his neck,' replied Sir Hugh shortly.

Mrs Carpenter had slept badly. Surely by now King Sol must have received an answer from Hugh, to say nothing of a substantial portion of that ridiculous ransom! What was he up to? Hatching some plan for extorting the full amount? He was probably consulting that mysterious Dr Santekul, who lived on the bank of the Big River and communed with tribal ancestors in the bush from time to time, just as the holy men of the Bible went into the desert whenever they felt the need of a spiritual boost. She felt rather feverish. A chill? Or perhaps 'flu? Then she diagnosed her ailment.

'I'm suffering from *suspense*!' she told herself aloud, and realised with dismay that she was developing this new habit of giving herself advice audibly as well as inwardly. 'I'm also suffering from claustrophobia and frustration,' she added irritably. 'Why won't these people let me go to the rock-pool in that torrent they call a river where the other women wash themselves and their clothes? Why won't King Sol allow me pencil and paper? Then I could write. I could really use this experience! Every illiterate criminal or captive cashes in on his story. Why not me? At least I wouldn't need a ghost-writer!'

She recalled the day King Sol had dictated the ransom letter to her. Here, in her hut, in the early afternoon. When it was written she had held onto the cheap writing-pad and the ball-point. But he had put out his hand for them.

'May I keep these?' she'd asked.

'I'm sorry.'

'I'm an author,' she'd pleaded. 'I need to exercise my mind and my craft, just as your palomino needs to gallop on the open veld with her mane and tail streaming in the wind.'

His laughter had rumbled to the thatch.

'You can observe as much as you like, but I regret, Mrs Carpenter, *no scribbling* except at my command. You must exercise other senses. Your memory must work for you instead of your pen, and your imagination can gallop far and wide, like my palomino on the right territory. But tread carefully in the paths of our minds. You might find the going there strange and not so good.'

She had placed the pad and ball-point in the pale waiting palm, and, for the first time, she had really seen him as her gaoler. A mist, like a dark curtain, had fallen between them, shutting out the warmth and light of the friendship she had come to value.

'You are dreaming, Wise One,' said Dawn as she set down the clay bowl and jug of warm water as usual. 'It was not a good dream, I think. Your eyes were closed but your face was troubled.'

Mrs Carpenter looked up at the girl beside her bed.

'Yes,' she said. 'It was a dream – a dream of a dark curtain between me and the light.'

A touch of fear quickened in the black eyes that could be so expressive or, at times, so blank.

'Wake!' Dawn said. 'Shake the curtain away! Soon I will bring your mealie-pap and when you have washed and eaten you will go out into the sun. It is a fine fresh day.'

The whole darn situation's getting me down, thought Mrs Carpenter, as she washed and dressed in the costume she had come to take for granted. Something's bound to break today. It must or I'll go off my rocker! I've had enough of this harem existence.

She brushed her thick hair vigorously and felt a certain glow of satisfaction as her scalp tingled under the bristles. She'd do it a new way today. Anything for a change! She parted it in the middle and plaited the two sections so that they hung over her shoulders. Then she drew a few threads from her blanket and tied each plait, brushing and combing the ends. 'They look like a pair of fly-whisks,' she said as she let them fall over her bead collar. 'Eccentrically schoolgirlish for a dame of my age!'

The reflection improved her temper and she drew a long breath of sparkling mountain air as she emerged from her hut. The tethered goat watched her with its inimical yellow gaze as she prepared to take her daily constitutional, marching sturdily round the sprawling kraal and cattle byre, just inside the high thorn-fence which she now accepted as her prison wall. As usual, a number of children accompanied her, skipping and frolicking, and the old and young looked up from their duties or their gossip to nod and smile at her. She had become part of their daily lives – alien but agreeable – a visitor who had gone through various phases which they had noted with interest.

She had shown a certain bewilderment at first, like a strange dog unsure of its reception among the animals of the compound, but her nervousness had soon calmed down. Curiosity had taken its place as she began to copy their ways and words, teaching them hers in exchange. Then had followed a sort of group identification as she realised that she too was one of the King's subjects, under restraint yet privileged, an important person who had earned the sobriquet 'Wise One'. She had not hesitated to establish the fact that she had favourites like Dawn, who had become her handmaiden, and who fed her from the cook-pot of her sister. But she had soon come to realise that adults were cautious in their conversation with her. They talked *of* her a great deal, but *to* her guardedly. Solinje was different. He was still a child, though precocious, and it was recognised that he had become as precious to the Wise One as a first grandson, one to be indulged and admired. The women laughed among themselves and said that she danced to the tune called by his bamboo flute, and it amused them to see her shake the paw of the tick-ridden dog who was his shadow.

One fact the people found disturbing. They sensed that the Rain-Maker and the Wise One were hostile to each other. And this was bad. The kraal heaved a communal sigh of relief and relaxed every time the Rain-Maker took herself off for days on end, seeking herbs and strange creatures in the bush, roaming in the solitude that is essential to the sorcerer who must gather spell-binding ingredients while communing with ancestral ghosts, magical beings and animal familiars beyond the ken of ordinary people.

But of late it was whispered in the kraal that the King's guest was becoming worried and restless. Her spirit was no longer looking outwards. It had begun to turn in upon itself, and that, they knew, was dangerous. When a person ceased to be part of the life about her, he or she would eventually lie down and turn her face to the wall in the darkness of her hut. Was the Rain-Maker, or worse still, the Witch-doctor from the Big River, casting a spell upon the Wise One like slow poison? Isolating her? They found the thought chilling.

Mrs Carpenter paused in her walk exactly where her regular retinue of near-naked children expected. It had become their habit to clamber up the fence-pole there to see why she always stood so still at this particular point and looked upwards at the hillside as she did.

It was simple enough. Here the mountain-path from the torrent was visible against the sky and sometimes she was lucky enough to see the timeless African frieze of women – carriers of water or fire-wood – moving majestically in single file, their burdens crowning perfectly poised heads. Could any picture be more satisfying, more profoundly part of the earth itself?

Today the frieze was different.

The children fell like ripe apples from the fence into the dust and scattered with wild excited shouts and squeals. Within seconds the kraal was buzzing as every beehive hut disgorged its occupants, while those who were already outside ran to the entrance of the fence and flowed out onto the path beyond it to find out what was happening.

Mrs Carpenter, suddenly abandoned, stood quite still.

So this was it!

She watched the three horsemen silhouetted against the hot blue sky and within moments they were descending the home-track. The Rain-Maker awaited them outside her hut, all in white, with a high baboon-fur head-dress adding to her massive stature.

Mrs Carpenter heard the familiar turmoil of welcome and the shrill cries of the children as the palomino, tossing her impatient head, entered the kraal and high-stepped it to where the Rain-Maker stood.

King Solomon remained seated when he reined in the mare. There was no smile on his face today although he bent, as was his custom, to throw packets of sweets to the children who clustered round him. He wore a blue safari-suit and a sombrero with a snake-skin band on it. The children, awe-struck, were hesitant about catching the sweets or scrambling after them. They seemed gripped in the spell of the second rider who looked down upon them from his pale dappled nag.

My God! thought Mrs Carpenter, he looks for all the world like one of the Four Horsemen of the Apocalypse! ' . . . I beheld a pale horse: and his name that sat on him was Death and Hell followed. . . .'

Close behind this sinister figure was a groom on a dusty black pony. His eyes were riveted on his master from the Big River.

The Witch-doctor dismounted and stood very tall, his face narrow as an axe. He wore a white robe and a high white turban adorned by monkey fur. A baboon-skin bag was slung across one shoulder and a hunting-knife in a sheath over the other. His necklaces were of polished animal teeth and claws; monkey-tails hung from the bead belt round his waist, as did the sign of his calling, an antelope horn. Strange and potent powders and medicaments were contained in that horn. He tossed a tin to his colleague, the Rain-Maker, who caught it with a nod of satisfaction.

'Probably snuff,' Mrs Carpenter said to herself, but, like the children who had failed to pick up their sweets, she was hypnotised by the stranger. She noticed that the groom had taken the reins of the pale horse, and that Solinje stood by his father's palomino. She saw his small dark hand fondle the restless satin nose of the 'golden horse'. He looked up suddenly in answer to some order brusquely given by the King and stood to attention. Then he turned and his eyes sought hers. He ran towards her, where she stood apart.

'Come, Wise One! My father, the King, asks for you.'

She followed the child and the crowd made way for them. Even the herd-boys had deserted the cattle in the grazing grounds except for one who remained on guard with dogs to support him. Soon one of his friends would relieve him.

They formed a small group outside the Rain-Maker's hut. Two more than life-size figures in white faced King Sol, who remained mounted. The groom and Solinje stood at the horses' heads.

Mrs Carpenter looked up at the King. He stared at her in astonishment and she smiled and touched the long plaits that hung over her shoulders. She bent a knee and then stood near Solinje, gently stroking the palomino's arched neck.

The King addressed her. 'You have heard of Dr Santekul, the famous herbalist from the Big River. He is with us today to consult the Rain-Maker. Soon now the rain-making ritual for this district takes place near the source of the river. On such important occasions the Rain-Maker and Dr Santekul work together.'

'Naturally.' She bowed to the Witch-doctor with a dignity that matched his own. 'I have heard of your powers, Dr Santekul.'

He returned the gesture gravely. 'And I have heard of your wisdom, lady.'

He was studying her frankly, his gaze intent, cold and penetrating.

Then it happened. The portent.

The mare whinnied and tossed her head. For an instant her mane seemed caught up with Mrs Carpenter's plaits and the midday sun made silver and gold of both. She ducked her head back quickly and was just in time to hear the Witch-doctor bark an order to the Rain-Maker, whose eyes signalled agreement. In the next instant Mrs Carpenter saw the flash of the small hunting-knife as Santekul drew it from its sheath and passed it to his colleague. The blade was bright and sharp as a surgeon's scalpel.

With incredible speed for so heavy a woman, the Rain-Maker lunged forward and seized the long fair plaits with their swinging tassels of bright soft hair. Two swift accurate strokes amputated one and then the other.

The King had drawn himself up in the saddle, towering above the Rain-Maker. She pushed one plait into her capacious baboon-skin bag, and the other, cupped in both open palms, she offered to King Solomon. He accepted it as if mesmerised. Its sun-heat and human warmth seemed to scald his flesh. He pressed the braided hair quickly out of sight into the flap-pocket of his safari-jacket. It was the old magic – the material symbol for which he had been waiting – but it gave him little pleasure as it lay snake-like against his hip.

Mrs Carpenter felt no pain. There was none to feel in the lightning assault. But there was sensation and intense shock. She had been humiliated in the presence of those who stood, staring and dumbfounded. She had been, metaphorically speaking, decapitated at the feet of the King. She was pale and weak, as if her blood were flowing out of her veins into the dust under her cowhide sandals. She saw Dawn and the Little Queen bury their faces in their hands, and, beside her, she knew that Solinje stood as if frozen into a small bronze statue of horror.

They all knew what it meant. Everybody. Even the children.

The strength had gone out of the White Wise One. In this hour of high noon Mrs Carpenter had been condemned to a sacrificial death.

King Solomon entered her hut within the hour.

She was ready for him, her shorn head swathed in the large *doek* Dawn had left on her bed, unasked and deeply understanding. Mrs Carpenter had used the printed black and white material well. She had folded it softly and built it tall and steeple-shaped to add dignity to its wearer. Her loose blanket, leaving one shoulder bare, fell impressively to her ankles and the deep beaded bib with its patterned message of welcome accentuated the length and pride of her withered neck. Her face had grown gaunt in the past weeks but the people with whom she now had to deal respected age, confusing it with the acquired wisdom of long experience, which so often leaks away with passing years.

Solinje and his dog were not with the King any more. They had returned to the herds. The King stood alone in his captive's hut confronting an unfamiliar adversary, a stranger who neither bent the knee nor appeared pleased to see him.

Mrs Carpenter waited for him to speak.

He strode silently across to the wooden table where Dawn would place Mrs Carpenter's bowl of food. He slapped down the brief-case he carried with him and drew up the *riempie* chairs. Then he opened the brief-case and took out two letters, one typed, one written in Jane's neat hand. Lastly he laid a manilla envelope on the table and placed upon it the supple blonde and silver braid, its severed end sealed with a neat elastoplast dressing. Mrs Carpenter looked at it with contemptuous distaste. He motioned her to be seated. She ignored the gesture.

'Sit down and read those letters for yourself,' he commanded. 'There is one from the British Ambassador to your captors, and a short personal note to you from your grand-daughter. I have, of course, examined them both already.'

A shaft of sunlight streamed through the open doorway. She carried the letters to the light.

Her son-in-law's communication to the kidnappers, on official Embassy notepaper, was brief and to the point.

> This is a first instalment, one tenth of the million rands demanded. A second instalment will follow when I receive evidence that the hostage is alive and well.
>
> It is impossible to pay the full sum immediately, as both the British and the South African Governments refuse to contribute, and (as Mrs Carpenter can inform you) the hostage's personal fortune has been invested for her family in unbreakable trusts.
>
> If Mrs Carpenter can suggest *any* legal way in which the required sum can be immediately borrowed, or otherwise obtained and transferred, I will, of course, put her instructions into effect without delay.
>
> Signed: Hugh Etheridge.

The King was watching her closely. As she folded her son-in-law's letter and passed it back to him he observed an enigmatic expression on her face which made it appear both cunning and remote.

In fact, Maud Carpenter was well satisfied. Hugh was toeing the line – *her* line! He had kicked the ball neatly into her court and she could now prove her faith in Clause 5 of her own Creed. Or she could change her mind and disclose the means of paying out in full.

She unfolded the second letter. It was addressed to 'Maud Carpenter'. Janie, she thought. Oh, dear Janie, don't weaken me!

> . . . Everything I possess is yours, but it's chicken-feed against the kidnappers' demands. Dream up some way we can raise the money! *You can and you must!* Don't you realise the world needs you. You give people distraction and entertainment. You even understand why good men and women may do things that seem very evil, because, dear Gran, you have the magical gift of a thinking heart.
>
> Your Janie.

As Mrs Carpenter folded the letter, the King saw that she was far away. He put out his hand for it, but she neither noticed nor responded.

'The letter, please, Mrs Carpenter. You'll have an opportunity of answering it later today.'

She handed it to him without replying. Her cheeks were sunken and her eyes hollow. She heaved a deep sigh but her features were lightened by a secret smile. Jane was very near her at that moment. 'Dear Janie,' she murmured under her breath. 'Always so generous and impulsive. But that last sentence, written with love, may well have cooked my goose! Not to worry, it was probably cooked anyway. . . .'

'Did you say something?' asked the King, frowning.

She looked up at him, the half smile still lingering on her lips.

'Perhaps I was thinking aloud, King Sol. Hostages are lonely people. They develop strange habits, as you may have noticed.'

10
'You must stay, Mr Obito. We may need your help . . .'

Abelard Cain let out the blue and white spinnaker, made it fast, and felt the buoyant thrust of Yates's yacht 'Sea-Sprite' as the great balloon filled and carried them, wind-borne, along the coast.

'Man, this is the life!'

Yates, at the helm, smiled. 'You must miss it in your land-locked country. Where did you learn your sailing?'

'Newport. When I was at Harvard.'

'I've never been to America.' Yates spoke regretfully.

'You've plenty of time,' put in Kim, lounging against the mast, a can of beer in his hand. 'Diplomats get around no end.'

'Come to that, isn't it time you got around and took the helm for a bit?'

Kim moved over and Desmond called down the hatch, 'What about some sandwiches, Janie? Oh, and catch, will you!' He stripped off his jersey and tossed it down to her.

When she came on deck, she was carrying a platter of sandwiches and sausage-rolls on a bed of curly lettuce. Her firm, near-naked body was deeply tanned. A beautiful shape, thought Kim, long-limbed and well balanced, moving gracefully to the lilt of 'Sea-Sprite'. Enough to turn any man on! But, to his surprise, he noticed that Cain, even as he helped himself to lettuce and a sandwich, was scarcely aware of Jane. The young

Nyangreelan's attention was riveted on the muscular bare torso and lacerated left arm of Yates.

'Say, Desmond, that's a fine see-through dressing on your arm! You been tangling with a mighty fierce cat?'

'Quite a tattoo,' agreed Yates, glancing down at the three raw scars emphasised by recently removed stitches.

Farrar noticed that Cain's bronze face was grave as he said: 'Like to talk about it?'

'No thanks. We're going to anchor in that cove under the cliffs and swim ashore from the yacht. Salt water is recommended for this sort of scratch, so if a drop or two penetrates the dressing, which is guaranteed waterproof, who cares?'

'I do,' said Jane.

'Not to worry,' Abelard told her. 'I'd soon put him right by borrowing a few drops of our Rain-Maker's special panacea – cold water taken from the cold ocean at full tide under a full moon.'

Jane looked at him in surprise. 'You said that last bit as if you were reciting a spell! I believe you're really superstitious at heart.'

He opened a can of beer as he answered. 'Who isn't? Everybody has different superstitions, that's all. Ours are elemental, of course, and there's ancestor worship in our philosophy. As for yours – variations on the theme of heaven and hell. This period is a flourishing one for Satan, I'm told. Witches fly over the green pastures of England, black masses are celebrated in medieval cathedrals while the deathwatch beetles gnaw ancient woodwork to dust and the effigies of crusaders, with their wives beside them and their dogs at their feet, sleep calmly under stained-glass windows. *They* don't give a damn! They've seen it all before – vandalism, torture and murder in the name of religion. People haven't changed all that much, Jane. They want their gods powerful and frightening, jealous and hungry – with a taste for human sacrifice.'

'Nice rhetoric!' said Kim. 'But you've elevated superstition to religion.'

Abelard's eyes swept his audience of three. It seemed to him that he caught a trace of hostility in their faces. He laughed. 'Don't take me seriously. With us witches are always on the job, and the ancestors rest lightly with one eye on their descendants. As for the old gods, yours or ours, they're like the rest of us, they enjoy a barbecue with, at times, some very fancy frills.'

Yates bent to let go the anchor and Abelard's 'fancy frills' were lost in the rattle of the anchor-chain and the cries of gulls. Jane helped him lower the mainsail and Abelard folded down the flapping spinnaker to make a neat stow.

The cove was small and deserted, well protected by massive rocks on either side of the little silver beach. The sheer flowering cliffs formed a natural backdrop to an intimate retreat more easily approached from the sea than the land.

Kim found a moment to say quietly to Yates: 'Take Jane one way and I'll guide Abelard in the opposite direction. I want to talk to him alone. It'll mean confidence for confidence. Give us time.'

'Anything you learn must be shared – '

'We three are in this business together. That was established in Johannesburg. And naturally H.E. is head of the team. I fancy we may need some high-powered diplomacy. You must accept my judgment.'

'Right. You may be sure Jane and I will go along with whatever you decide. H.E. is impressed with the way you've handled – and muzzled – the media.'

As Jane and Desmond swam for the shore leisurely side by side, she said: 'Abelard guesses something . . . something that scares him.'

'Kim thinks so too. Whatever it is, he means to do a bit of probing. He doesn't want us around. He tipped me off to keep you out of the way.'

She laughed. 'I'm not complaining.'

She was treading water, feeling the lift of the tide caressing her bare limbs. He was beside her, his hands on her waist. He could touch the firm sand with the soles of his feet now, but she was still out of her depth. He drew her towards him, lifting her till her cheek was against his and his own footing sure and strong to resist the scalloped surf lapping against them. In a couple of hours the wavelets would be breakers, but not yet. The gentle ebb and flow was a rhythm to which their bodies danced, skin to skin, her long dark hair clinging to his neck as if to bind them closer in strange ecstatic sea-loving.

When they stepped onto the beach, Kim and Abelard were already out of sight, their footprints leading away towards the far boulders.

Desmond took Jane's hand and they wandered towards the sun-hot grass at the base of the cliff screened by heath and rocks. They lay side by side, Jane totally relaxed, face to the sun, eyes closed.

'You know something, Janie?'

'What?' She spoke drowsily.

'Your face right now is a flower with dew on it.'

'And when did you see a dewy sunbaked flower?'

'Last spring among the Namaqualand daisies – '

'Being devoured by horse-flies.'

'The daisies didn't care.'

'I bet *you* did! Those flies draw blood. But I'll grant you the flower-fields are glorious – every colour, shape and size swaying in the breeze, happy together. The way the whole world ought to be.'

'This minute my whole world is us – you and me. Janie, can you even begin to guess how lovely you are?'

'Your salty sea-sprite, second favourite to her namesake out there beyond the surf.'

She turned her head to look at him, smiling and sensuous. She ran her fingers idly through his damp ruffled hair, glinting bright as it dried. His eyes, sweeping the lazy length of her limbs, were filled with rapture and the mist of desire. The smile left her parted lips and she felt her heart begin to pound as his hand moved gently over the smooth curves of her body. She closed her eyes and moved closer to him.

'Promise me,' he said, 'promise I'm the only one.'

Her mouth was dry as she answered, 'I swear it.'

'That night in Jo'burg? You and Kim alone. . . .'

She tried to draw away, but he held her tight.

'Des! I'm not that sort.'

'Don't ever be!' There was a fierce mastery in his passion now. She heard him whisper 'I'd kill for you!' and she was glad, lost in a storm of mounting sensation, shared and intensified, till the high peak of total possession made them one with each other and with the sky, sea and strong wild air.

'So that's the whole story to date, Abelard,' said Kim. 'All I know of it, anyway. I was at the Embassy on the Monday night that Elias, the butler, was mauled by the Leopard-Man who brought the ransom note. That was three weeks after the Carpenter kidnapping. We then followed all the instructions of the kidnappers, as I told you – '

'With that one important exception you mentioned. When Yates carried that brief-case to the rendezvous the sum it contained was only a fraction of the total sum demanded.'

Abelard sat with his arms clasping his knees and his back against a smooth boulder. He wore nothing except a beautifully beaded flat necklace that fell to his heart. His face was thoughtful and troubled. This was not the cheerful gambler and playboy, but a responsible young man confronted with a difficult problem. He looked at

Farrar who was running the fine white sand through his fingers as he sprawled on his side, back to the sun.

'Why have you taken me into your confidence, Kim?'

'I hoped that as August Obito, Director of Nyangreelan Intelligence, you might somehow be able to help us. We should hear from the kidnappers any time now – '

'You think they might be a Nyangreelan gang?'

'It's probable. The river ford near the baobab tree is right near the border between the Republic and Nyangreela.'

'The river borders three other territories adjoining the Republic.'

'I know, but the others are dominated by various Marxist terror organisations. Nyangreela is not – as yet. She is not multitribal. There'll be no genocide there. Your country is still a place of peace – the land of a united people.'

'Your Ambassador shares your opinion. When I called on him he made that clear. I'll make all possible investigations, I assure you.'

Abelard's handsomely carved face had assumed a certain expression Kim knew well. The blinds are down, he thought. We're on treacherous ground. I'm onto something, that's for sure. And so is he. But what? And who? He persevered.

'H.E. is expecting you to an informal dinner tonight. Just Desmond, you, me and the family. I'd like you to see the photostats of the correspondence between the kidnappers and H.E. before you meet him. I have them on board and I'll give them to you when we drop you at your Consulate. That way you'll be fully briefed before we meet this evening.'

Abelard groaned a protest. 'Man, I'm on vacation, pure and simple. Am I forced to become involved in Jane's grandmother's misfortunes?'

Kim took a chance. 'I think so. You see, I don't believe your vacation is all that . . . pure and simple. I have a hunch that someone high up prefers not to have you at home in your official capacity just now. Could this be a strategic holiday?'

Abelard's head shot up so sharply that Kim guessed he had touched a live nerve. He prodded deeper.

'If I'm right in thinking along those lines, it would have to be someone very high up indeed.'

'Like the Rain-Maker, who's run out of salt water from the cold sea – the sort of ice-cold that will make the clouds huddle together, like a flock of sheep, till they spill the much needed rain on our pastoral land.' Abelard laughed shortly, but now Kim's expression had become inscrutable.

'Your Rain-Maker needs her magical ingredients and you tell me your only chore here is to provide the one that can't be obtained in your own country with no access to the sea. I've been trying to figure out what other foreign ingredients she might want – for other mystical rites perhaps.'

'Don't overtax your imagination!'

Abelard sprang to his feet, lithe and dangerous. His gaze swept the sheltering cliff as he tried to regain his composure. Kim was amazed to see how quickly he succeeded in switching from a sensitive subject to neutral ground.

'Look who's there!' He pointed. 'Right above us. I thought you said our talk would be private.'

Sitting, solitary and attentive, on a high sundrenched ledge, was the biggest baboon either of them had ever seen. The animal's attention was riveted on the cove.

'That's the sentinel on his lookout-post. If we'd been having a picnic he'd have given a signal and the whole troupe would have come leaping down to join us. It's forbidden to feed them, but people go on doing it just the same.'

'Do you?'

'Certainly not. I respect authority, especially when it's dictated by good sense.'

'Uh-huh?'

'The whole of Cape Point is a Nature Reserve. Baboons are destructive as well as greedy and this troupe is very cheeky. But, up to a point, it's a great attraction. The baboons are like clever naughty children, very human. Fun to study.'

'Amusing till they become dangerous? Still, real humans are the most dangerous of all – thinking animals – the intruders here who've decided to colonise baboon territory and stock it with other wild creatures to add to its charms as a sanctuary.'

Kim turned to Abelard. 'I wish I had a girlfriend who'd make me a necklace with its secret love-message and give me a good luck charm to hang on it.'

Abelard touched the sunwarmed beads and his white teeth shone in a proud smile. 'She's very young and rather gorgeous, quick to learn too. We're going to be married in a few weeks' time.'

'Where will you live?'

'We've taken a pretty house with a garden quite near the Hydro-Casino. What about you? Surely you've a wife and family some place.'

'No place! I must be free to come and go. No ties.'

Yet, as he spoke, a vivid gypsy face rose to haunt him. Dark windswept hair, laughing eyes, sparkling one moment and deep in troubled thought the next, supple desirable body. Damn young Desmond! What was he up to right now? Not wasting his opportunity, that was sure.

'Well?' grinned Abelard. 'You've wandered a long way from this cove, haven't you?'

Kim started, then deliberately cooled down and allowed the unbidden flame of jealousy to burn out.

'Actually, I was very much in this cove.' He pointed up the steep cliff face. 'Take a glance at our friend up there. The old sentinel is still keeping us under strict supervision! He hasn't moved.'

'He won't worry us if we don't worry him. Baboons, as you remarked, are very human. Inquisitive, but on their guard. Only two things really scare them. A snake. And a leopard. They know those two to be killers.'

Kim's muscles tensed. Was Abelard giving him an oblique warning? It could well be so. He shaded his eyes with his hands as he turned and looked seawards. The slap of waves on the beach had grown much stronger during the past hour and the deep boom of the rising sea echoed from the rocky flanks of the cove.

'Time we rejoined "Sea-Sprite",' he said. 'The other two are back on board already. I can see them. Let's beat it, Abelard. The tide is flowing fast.'

It was cool and fresh on the terrace. Elias had taken the coffee tray and bidden the six people goodnight.

'We won't need you again,' the Ambassador had said, and turned to Abelard. 'On Saturday night the staff enjoy a get-together with their friends, so we see that it's not a party night here.'

Kirsty, who had returned from kennels the day before, lay with her chin on Jane's foot. Suddenly, as if electrified, she growled and sat up. The next moment she was tearing across the lawn, barking furiously.

Mabel Etheridge laughed.

'Back to duty for Kirsty! *The Argus* is delivered late on Saturdays up here – nine-thirty at best – and Kirsty feels it imperative to harass the newsboy before he has time to mount his bike and flee.'

Yates pulled Jane to her feet. She was relaxed after the day's yachting, eyes dreamy.

'Come on, before you doze off! We'll rescue the newsboy and

fetch the paper from the letter-box.'

Abelard half rose to follow them and then thought better of it as they raced across the grass in pursuit of the dog.

Kim noted the Nyangreelan's impulse and the second thought that kept him on the terrace, and in the back of his mind a tiny red-light flashed some sort of warning.

It was some time before Jane and Desmond reappeared and Mabel caught her husband's eye as if to say 'I told you so!'

When they did, they were strolling, arm in arm, reluctant to leave the garden. The dog was chasing from shrub to shrub, ecstatic to be back on her homeground with her own people and excited at having renewed her harmless but satisfying feud with the Xhosa newsboy, who always shouted at her in his own language as vigorously as she barked in hers.

The Ambassador held out his hand. 'Let's see who's murdering who and where?'

But, as Yates silently passed him *The Argus*, Sir Hugh saw that there was a long manilla envelope with it. He handed the paper quietly to his wife and gave his attention to the envelope. It bore no stamp and was addressed in the familiar hand of Maud Carpenter. He balanced it in his palm, feeling its weight and frowning as he tried to gauge the contents. He seemed oblivious of the five pairs of eyes intent upon his reactions. He was obviously unwilling to open the kidnappers' communication, sensing some material and immediate menace.

Abelard broke the silence. He made no pretence of being unaware of the significance of the strange fat envelope so obviously delivered by hand. He rose and said formally:

'I must be leaving, Excellency. It's been a long day in the fresh air.'

Sir Hugh impaled him with an impersonal but deeply thoughtful look. At last he said:

'You must stay, Mr Obito. We may need your help to save a life.' It was the first time he had used Abelard's official name.

Kim too had risen. He was of a height with the Nyangreelan and their eyes met in an unmistakable challenge.

'Just before dinner,' he said, 'Jane and I went down to that letter-box in case *The Argus* had come a little earlier than usual. But it was empty.'

'So . . . ?' Abelard's voice was softly resonant.

'We were back at the house in good time to meet you when your Consul dropped you outside in the road. Desmond too was already here.'

'So . . . ?' repeated Abelard with heightened interest.

'So one might assume that the messenger who delivered Mrs Carpenter's letter – the writing on the envelope is clearly hers – might well be one of two people, the newsboy –'

'Or myself.'

'Exactly.'

Abelard smiled grimly. He held out his hand to the Ambassador.

'Allow me to open that letter, Excellency. Just in case it should contain an explosive device.'

The Ambassador placed the envelope in the extended palm. Abelard stood under the light. He took a tiny knife from his pocket, drawing it carefully from its snake-skin sheath. The blade flashed as he slit the envelope.

'There is a letter here,' he said calmly, and passed it to Sir Hugh. 'There is also something else.'

He withdrew a long sock-shaped canvas container from the envelope and felt the slight shift of its contents in the hollow of his palm.

Kim caught his breath. He saw the Adam's apple rise in Abelard's throat, and sensed the revulsion with which he touched the sock, closed by a draw-string. Kim had seen snakes transported like that, torpid when shaken out, and gradually coming to life. Lethal. Could a reptile be the guardian of a severed finger or ear?

'Be careful!' he whispered.

Abelard was standing, hypnotised by the white line painted down the length of the canvas container now lying limp across his wrist. The white mark of the sorcerer. He was shaken with ancient apprehensions and sweat broke on his brow and upper lip as he released the draw-string to shake out the bag.

Oh, my God, a yellow cobra! thought Kim as the gleaming attenuated shape slid out of its sock and landed on the terrace with a light thud.

Everybody drew back. Except Jane.

She darted under the barrier of Kim's swiftly outstretched arm and in a flash she stooped and picked up the long silver-gold braid lying so still at her feet.

'One of Gran's plaits!' She held it against her cheek and turned to Mabel who stood, pale and tense. 'Remember how sometimes she used to wear her hair in two plaits and wind them round her head like a crown? Just for a change, she'd do it, just for fun. She must be all right. This is her way of telling us!'

No one answered and Jane's eyes widened slowly in dismay. Desmond put his arm about her shoulders. The plait she held against her cheek was soft, supple and shining, but there was no human warmth in it.

11.
'You're no coward... but this braid frightens you!'

'It's very curious,' said the Ambassador. 'This undated letter is from Maud Carpenter to me. It doesn't appear to be dictated and is certainly in her own hand – as firm as ever – but somehow it doesn't ring quite true.'

He took off his spectacles and looked away from the others as if seeking an answer or an enemy in the starlit garden, his brows knitted above the rather prominent eyes.

Same scene, same company, thought Kim. But no violence to add terror to the message. A very civilised messenger had replaced the Leopard-Man! Yet Kim was sure that Abelard had been genuinely shocked by the snake-like plait in the manilla envelope. He had touched it with nervous distaste, taken by surprise.

Desmond, leaning against the terrace balustrade, lit a cigarette for himself and one for Kim. Jane, who had placed the braid on the table, was perched on the arm of her stepmother's chair, while Sir Hugh, with the letter open on his lap, leaned forward in his rattan chair under the light. His half-smoked Havana burned in the slot of a large ceramic ashtray on the round glass-topped table at his side. He put out his hand for the iced whisky and water Yates had poured out for him. The mournful call of a night-bird and the distant barking of a dog were the only sounds that broke the silence.

The Ambassador set down his glass, replaced his spectacles and picked up the two sheets of closely-written cheap lined paper.

'This is what Maud Carpenter suggests. In fact, I have no option other than to carry out her wishes to the best of my ability. The instructions are set out in obvious collusion with her kidnapper.'

He read the letter with his usual careful deliberation.

'My dear Hugh,

In your communication, which accompanied the first instalment of the ransom, you asked me to suggest some "legal way" of paying the balance of the ransom without further delay. You also offered to put any suggestion I might make into immediate effect.

'I believe there *is* a solution to this problem, but it is one which will deprive Jane of her inheritance. However, her note to me was so warm and sincere that I do not hesitate to take this – the only way out. Please tell her how touched I was by all that she said in the note.

'The following are the instructions which my Captor insists should be carried out *with the utmost speed and discretion*.

'You must fly to Geneva and consult our good friend Baron X. I am sure that, knowing my life-or-death circumstances and, with your authority, he will arrange the transfer of my whole numbered account to another Swiss account to be opened for my Captor. The amount I have in my bank should just about cover the requisite sum. As the transfer documents will require my signature they will need to be brought here to me personally. As you know, so long as I am alive, only my own signature is valid.

'My Captor and I therefore want you to be accompanied on your journey by a trusted and competent young man who will make himself known to you. (He is, at present, unknown to *me*.) He will act on behalf of my Captor and bring the necessary documents to me for signing. When this has been done he will complete the transaction in Geneva.

'All this must be accomplished before Tuesday week, which is the *final deadline* (an unfortunate term!) for payment.

'On Wednesday week, at midnite, Desmond Yates and his helicopter pilot must come *together* to the same Baobab Rendezvous as before, where my Captor has promised I will be given into their care.

'Affectionately,
Maud C.'

Jane was the first to speak as the Ambassador folded the letter and put it on the glass-topped table next to him. Her eyes sparkled with excitement and hope.

'That's a genuine letter! How can you doubt it, Daddy? It's clear and concise and there's a characteristic touch – the bit about . . .' She broke off suddenly, as if the impact of the three words in parenthesis had only just struck her.

'Thank God she hasn't lost her spirit!' said Mabel. 'At last we can all feel that something really will be done to release Maud.'

The tide of hope and relief swept over Desmond. He took a step towards Abelard.

'Am I right in thinking "the trusted and competent young man" is with us here at this moment?'

The Nyangreelan smiled suddenly, relieving the gloom that had settled on his features since the opening of the manilla envelope. He bowed his head to the Ambassador.

'Excellency, Mrs Carpenter's letter has blown my cover. I have been chosen to go with you to Geneva. Our air-tickets have already been booked for tomorrow and your friend, Baron Weber, has been alerted. He hopes that you will be his house-guest while you are in Geneva.'

Kim noted the dangerous gleam in Sir Hugh's eyes as he said with deceptive calm:

'Routine tasks of that sort are usually assigned to my own staff.'

'Could you, for the present, sir, consider me as seconded to your staff?'

'By your country's Government, Mr Obito?'

'By my own Department, Excellency.'

The Ambassador rose and confronted the Nyangreelan. What splendid actors they are! thought Kim. The arrogant young African and the English aristocrat so well versed in the dubious ways of diplomacy.

'Then kindly make a third booking for my Second Secretary and let me have a schedule of our proposed movements during the next few days . . . and after.'

He made a gesture of dismissal, but his wife's voice claimed his attention.

'Hugh! Shouldn't we call Colonel Storr and let him know these new developments?'

'No,' answered the Ambassador decisively. 'What has happened tonight is not to be handed to the news media either. Nothing is to be released until I give the word. Is that understood, Kim?'

'Of course, sir.'

Sir Hugh's icy gaze focused on Abelard.

'In the present crisis Colonel Storr's hands are effectively tied. Even if he suspected our guest here of actually *being* the kidnapper Maud Carpenter refers to throughout her letter as "my Captor", he could not make an arrest without endangering the life of the hostage. The same applies to anyone acting on behalf of the Captor in question.'

'Substitute the word *terminating* for *endangering* and His Excellency's assessment of the situation is accurate,' said Abelard. He turned to his hostess. 'If you'll excuse us, Lady Etheridge, Desmond and I must discuss the arrangements. His Excellency's task is important – crucial, in fact – and our time is short.'

Jane sprang to her feet.

What now? wondered Kim, as she took the plait from the coffee-table and offered it to Abelard.

'You and Desmond will require this for your Carpenter file.'

He flinched and drew back.

'I have no file. Give it to Desmond!'

His voice had risen in pitch and she stood for a moment, as if to watch the sweat break out on his upper lip and forehead. Then she said quietly:

'You're no coward, Abelard, but this braid frightens you! I wonder why?'

Sunday dawned, crisp and sunny, but to Jane it was a dislocated day, full of tensions. She felt isolated and un-needed. Her father was in his study with Des and Abelard working out an itinerary which would enable them to accomplish their Swiss mission as speedily as possible. This afternoon they would be on their way. Kim was writing up his endless notes on the Carpenter case and had gone to the Chancery to do so.

'There are things I want to look up in the Embassy archives,' he'd announced that morning at breakfast. 'I'll be working in the library.'

'The librarian will be off duty,' Lady Etheridge had pointed out, but he had only smiled.

'Thanks for the reminder but I know my way about the archives. In fact, we're all contributing to them right now.'

She had nodded, and soon afterwards had settled down to the dull but necessary business of making last minute decisions about household packing for the move to Pretoria. That left Jane to her own devices. She decided to spend the morning with Maud Carpenter's 'Personal Problems' journal.

With Kirsty at her heels, she wandered down the garden to her favourite umbrella pin-oak and settled herself beneath it on a light wicker chaise-longue with a little garden-table beside it.

She felt very tired and realised that a strong reaction to the events of the past few weeks had set in. Too much had happened to her grandmother, and so to her and to her father who looked gaunt with worry.

For a while she lay back, gazing up into the red-green tracery of delicate foliage already touched with early autumn. When she had arrived less than two months ago those slender branches had offered a canopy of radiant green. Now the first parchment-pale leaves fluttered gently onto the grass, so weightless that even Kirsty did not move when a few settled on her coat.

Jane closed her eyes and scenes were re-enacted in her mind like a closed–circuit television complete with soundtrack. They went back to her arrival at D.F. Malan Airport.

Desmond had met her, and, from that moment, he had seen her differently, no longer as the teenage daughter of his chief, but as a young woman with a job and personality of her own. His deceptively innocent green eyes had opened even wider than usual and his manner towards her had changed subtly. Masterful he had always been in a bantering way, but soon she had sensed a heightened possessiveness in his attitude.

It was he who had fetched her from the tennis-court the afternoon her father had heard of the snatch. She'd been playing in a girls' four. He'd interrupted it brusquely.

'Jane, you're wanted in the study. H.E. has something important to tell you.'

One of the two sitting out had taken her place and she'd hurried to the study with Des. Her father and Mabel were waiting for them.

Her father's face was taut and troubled.

'I've just had a telephone call from Marula Police Station. Your grandmother has disappeared. Probably kidnapped. Colonel Storr, the Chief of the Peninsula Robbery and Murder Squad, is on his way here now.'

She'd felt sick and her racquet had clattered onto the polished floor between the Persian rug and the desk. Des had picked it up and Mabel had said:

'Are you all right, Jane?'

Des had pushed a chair forward but she'd shaken her head. Every sound was magnified. The scrape of the chair had pulled her together. It was very odd. In her mind she'd clearly heard Maud Carpenter's voice.

'The police will scratch about among my papers. *Don't let them get my confidential journal*. Hide it, Janie! Hide it!'

'Jane!' Mabel had repeated. 'Are you all right?'

'Yes,' she'd answered. 'But I'm going to the bathroom. I'll be back in a minute.'

She'd dashed upstairs and, to her relief, Mabel hadn't followed her. She knew her grandmother's scribble-books and folders swollen with news cuttings and plots for her thrillers. Since she'd been a schoolgirl Maud Carpenter had discussed them with Jane as if they were equals. 'It's a game between us,' she'd said. 'The Imagination Stimulant. We toss ideas back and forth – good for us both.' But there was one journal even Jane dared not touch. It was labelled *Personal Problems*. Once she'd picked it up and turned a page, but her grandmother had taken it from her.

'*Not that one*, Janie! It's private, my own affair.' She'd added more gently and rather sadly: 'One day bits of it may be your affair. Not yet, my child.'

'When?'

'When I'm not able to stop you reading it. That day it'll be *yours*. Don't forget! You'll know by instinct when that day comes.' 'That day' had come and the journal was hers. She'd read it avidly.

More than once.

She sighed now as she riffled through the pages again, seeking some new answer. A way out.

The record went back a long way to the days when her grandfather, John Carpenter, had been the Squire of the Sussex village that was the scene of so many Maud Carpenter thrillers. Jane had lived with her grandparents after her mother's death, and later the 'big house' had once again been her home during school holidays. She could still hear the peacocks screeching over the Georgian rooftop and walled garden in the dawn and then the different calls of the birds.

There were two entries in the journal that drew her like magnets. These were, Jane realised, 'her affair'.

The first was written in her parents' home in Athens shortly after her birth. Ann Carpenter was an excellent linguist and a classical scholar who, before her hasty marriage to Hugh Etheridge, had been employed in the typing pool at the British Embassy. Soon after Jane's birth Maud Carpenter had flown to Athens.

> . . . I arrived too late for the baby's birth. Jane was due in July and here she is in May! I flew to Greece a fortnight after Hugh telephoned us. He said Ann and the infant were both flourishing though of course Jane was premature and tiny. It would be best, he said, to have me to stay when Ann and Jane were home from the hospital. They would need me then.
>
> My John was sweet about letting me go and the old biddies in the village have all promised to take good care of him. In any case I shan't be needed here for long as Ann and Hugh have an excellent Greek couple who have identified themselves with this young family. It is, I gather, considered 'chic' to manage the household of a diplomat if the price is right! Luckily it is, as Hugh has a handsome private income with a great deal more to

follow when his father dies and he inherits 'The Ridge' in Cumberland and the baronetcy. He is the sole heir.

I had never set eyes on my son-in-law until the day before yesterday when he met me on my arrival. He's very distinguished-looking in his austere way, a tall young man, clean-shaven, fairish with most arresting grey eyes and really beautiful hands – I always notice hands – and I can imagine that his would be very sensitive on the reins of a horse. And with a woman too, no doubt! He's a fine all-round sportsman, quite a gambler too, I'm told, and yet there's something inhibited about him. I find him a 'so far and no further' sort of person.

He's obviously deeply in love with Ann. And she loves him. There's a difference. She's blooming and is adorable with her baby.

'Our life will take us all over the world,' she said to me this morning when we were on the patio with Jane in her pram. 'Our daughter will be able to go with us and get her schooling wherever we may happen to be. So much easier than a boy.'

I looked at my first grandchild and said: 'Wasn't Hugh disappointed not to have a son? I mean, he is the last of a long line – the fourteenth baronet – '

'No,' she cut in quickly. 'There's plenty of time for sons.'

'You didn't waste much time over this child, did you?'

She raised that shining fair head on its long neck and gave me a comical wry look.

'I've been expecting that crack.'

Jane's pram was beside me, and I lifted one of those miniature dimpled hands so that the strong Greek sunlight shone on the perfectly formed nails.

'If this is a premature baby, then I'm not a day over thirty.'

She laughed in that infectious way of hers, eyes dancing, totally unrepentant.

'Then you've solved the mystery of our little early bird. Clever old Mum! I didn't think we'd get away with the premature story.'

'You're a brazen hussy!'

'Just badly brought up and rather ignorant. Your fault.'

'All the same, there *is* a mystery,' I said.

She raised her eyebrows, and the baby blew a bubble.

'Tell!'

'It's Hugh. I only met him two days ago, and, although he's a dashing young man, I can't see him as a seducer.'

'Seducer? For Pete's sake, Mum, pull up your socks! There's no such creature outside the covers of Edwardian fiction. And Hugh's no rapist either!'

'Well then, what happened?'

'Need you ask?' Ann's face was still alight with amusement. But quite suddenly she took pity on me. 'It was – let's stay with the Edwardians – love at first sight for Hugh. He gave me that terrific long look the first time I was fished out of the typing-pool to do some work for him, and after that he saw to it that I was allocated to him for all his work. One way and another we spent most of our time together that spring and, at the end of the summer, he asked me to marry him. But I wasn't sure of my own feelings. I had to make sure. There's only one way, isn't there?'

'All I can say is you were careless.' (Not enough instruction, I admitted inwardly. Yes, perhaps it *was* my fault!)

'Are you sorry?' Ann's eyes were on her baby.

'The child is a darling. How could I be sorry?'

The next entry which closely concerned Jane was more significant.

For three years her parents had been *en poste* abroad, so John and Maud Carpenter had seen very little of Ann and their granddaughter. When Jane was three Hugh took four months' furlough to settle the family estate which he had recently inherited at the death of his father, his only remaining relative.

Maud Carpenter noted the event in her journal with all its implications.

John and I stayed with the young couple and their little one at 'The Ridge' among the green hills and shining lakes of Cumberland. The child is fascinating, intelligent and affectionate, prone to tantrums but full of ready laughter too.

'She's not much like either of her parents,' I said to John. 'She's a gypsy changeling. That dark straight hair and those dancing brown eyes.'

'She's got Ann's temperament,' he said, 'and Hugh's fine features as far as one can tell at this age. But that's not exotic enough, is it? Flamenco for you, Maud!'

I think my dear husband finds my super-heated imagination rather trying at times. He and his son-in-law saw eye to eye on most matters. Only one thing jarred on John, who has an exaggerated sense of the territorial imperative. Every good squire has.

'Too much foreign service,' he said to me one evening. 'Hugh doesn't really appreciate this gorgeous Lake District and his own magnificent heritage.'

'Perhaps he's afraid of loving "The Ridge" too much,' I suggested.

Surprisingly, John didn't dismiss the possibility. 'He's the last of the Etheridge baronets. It's up to Ann to provide the heir.'

'She doesn't want to. She's content with Jane.'

He frowned. 'But it's her duty to try for a boy. You must convince her!'

'That's Hugh's job, not mine.' But I'm interfering by nature, so I took the bit between my teeth one day when we happened to be alone. Jane was having her morning nap in the nursery that led onto a little covered porch and a garden rambling down to the water's edge and the boathouse. John and Hugh were playing a round of golf.

I drew a long breath before tackling my daughter. She doesn't welcome criticism, however well-meaning. Never has.

'When are you going to give Jane a brother?'

It seemed ages before she answered and I looked up from the tapestry I was embroidering. She was weighing up the pros and cons. Should she tell me the truth or fabricate a story? I think it was then that I realised how badly I had failed to earn her full confidence. It was seldom volunteered. Perhaps all her life she had resented my absorption in my work – my fantasy world which excluded her. So, by denying me her own realities, she adjusted the balance. At last she said:

'There'll be no more babies for Hugh and me.' The way she declared it was quite final.

'But why not? You had an easy confinement and Jane is a healthy lovely child.'

She turned to me with a half sigh.

'Share it then, Mummy, if you must – the fly in the ointment of a happy marriage. Hugh had a vasectomy a few weeks before Jane was born. That means he can make love – oh, *that* part of our marriage is fine – but he can't make babies any more.'

'But why? Why on earth should he have done such a thing?'

'For a very good reason indeed. There's a genetic flaw in the Etheridge family. It may skip a few generations, but it's there. Have you heard of Crouzon's Disease?'

'Yes. Children born with facial – and possibly other – deformities that make them . . . rather horrifying to look at.'

'It makes them outcasts – poor little souls – and they are

often very highly intelligent and sensitive, so their suffering is doubled. These days they can undergo plastic surgery. After years of hoping and suffering and many operations, they *may* come out presentable, but with a thousand hang-ups. Life is hard enough for normal people without intolerable congenital handicaps in an overpopulated world. So, you see, I agree entirely with Hugh's action.'

'Did he tell you of this . . . flaw in his family history *before* – '

Ann cut in fast, with heightened colour. 'Jane was an accident, as you know. When I realised I was pregnant I told Hugh. He was very understanding, very sweet – ' Her voice shook a little as she went on. 'He told me everything then. And he left the choice to me. Marry him and have my baby. Or procure an abortion and my freedom. You could fix that at a price and Hugh could well afford it.'

'Why didn't you follow that alternative course?'

'I'm a normal woman. I wanted my baby desperately . . . and I loved Hugh. I wanted him too.'

'So you chanced it?'

'The risk was minimal, and I felt – I *knew* – the child I carried had a right to life.'

She sprang up as if to forbid further questioning. 'Time Jane woke up. I'm going to the nursery.'

She left me on the porch, cold with shock. Not for Ann's sake or Hugh's, but for Jane's. One day the same choice would be hers. A childless marriage, or to take the 'minimal risk' that might spell tragedy for a human being whose 'right to life' would depend on her decision.

Jane let her head fall back against the cushioned headrest of the wicker chair and the journal slid from her lap onto the grass. As had happened so many times since she had read and re-read the journal, she had found it deeply upsetting to analyse the sublimated mother-figure she had worshipped all her life and had now begun to criticise so cruelly.

Only yesterday, in the cove she and Des had come to regard as their own, he had told her that he wanted to marry her – 'for keeps, Janie. Just being lovers isn't good enough. Oh, it's wonderful, but don't you understand that you and I belong to each other every way there is for a man and woman?'

'Isn't this every way?' she'd pleaded. 'I love you.' Don't let's spoil it, she'd thought. Let's have this! But he'd persisted.

'Then marry me and share my life properly – every bit of it that's humanly possible! A home of our own and – one day – a family.'

'Not yet!' She'd leapt up and raced down to the sea. He'd caught her up and held her to him. Desire had flamed again, cutting out further argument before they swam back to 'Sea-Sprite'.

She'd felt a cheat, even then, not to have told him the truth. Later, she'd thought, later I will! We'll find some way out. At least now if you start a baby and have any reason to think it mightn't be healthy or normal there's a time when the specialists can tell you . . . and take it away. And after a while – centuries perhaps – I believe these bad hereditary genes wither and die. Maybe ours have done that. She groped, in a bewildered turmoil, for a solution, while all the time, deep down, she bitterly resented that she had been kept in ignorance. It had been her father's duty to tell her instead of letting her learn by accident from Maud Carpenter's journal.

'When he comes back from Switzerland I'll put him through the third degree,' she whispered to herself. 'You wait, Daddy, just you wait!'

12

'The old cults ride again...'

Jane insisted on going to the airport to see her father off with Desmond and Abelard that afternoon. The Ambassador wanted no protocol at the airport. Not even Kim.

'You'll ring me from Switzerland tomorrow night?' Jane begged him.

'Of course,' agreed Sir Hugh. 'Des or I will keep in touch.'

Meanwhile Kim and Mabel Etheridge relaxed by the pool after a swim.

'That was wonderfully refreshing,' she said. 'But I feel it's working up for a storm. Or perhaps it's just my own pent-up tension.'

She took off the shower-cap she'd worn for her dip and shook out her shining brown hair. Her generous contours were controlled by a cleverly elasticised bathing-suit. She's a healthy-looking matron, Kim thought. So different from the filly! Well, there's no blood relationship. Will Jane ever lose that mettlesome look of hers? Maybe, after a couple of kids. I doubt it, though. He answered his hostess.

'It's tension, Lady Etheridge. We've all been on edge for quite a while.'

'Have you put out a press release?'

'Yes. Brief and misleading, but necessary. The Ambassador can't go flying off to Europe without arousing comment. So we've said and I quote: "The British Ambassador, Sir Hugh Etheridge, accompanied by his Second Secretary, Mr Desmond Yates, is flying to London to make arrangements for expediting the payment of the full ransom demanded by the kidnappers of Mrs Maud Carpenter. Her whereabouts and the identity of her kidnappers is still unknown, but she is believed to be in good health and well treated." Unquote.'

He added with a grin, 'The paragraph can be used *after* the party arrive in Geneva.'

'I see. The story is to appear to be London-based. Abelard isn't mentioned?'

'Indeed not. We don't want to involve Nyangreela.'

'And Colonel Storr? What does he know?'

'He knows, in confidence, that it's Geneva. "A precaution," Sir Hugh has told him. "To ensure that the next demand can be met."'

Mabel sighed. 'We know so little ourselves. How did your library investigations go this morning?'

'Well enough. There were a lot of old files I wanted to consult.'

'And you found them?'

'With no trouble. They were all together, and they'd been studied recently. I realised the Ambassador had been covering the same ground that interested me. As perhaps you already know?'

Her eyes were inexpressive behind her dark glasses.

'Hugh is cagey about the distribution of news as you've sometimes complained. Please tell me a little of what *you* ferreted out.'

'I'm sure you'll keep what I tell you to yourself. On no account must Jane get wind of it. She'd have nightmares.'

Mabel took off her glasses to look at him and he found himself embarrassed and a little touched at the gratitude in her expression. He'd felt all along that she'd been too much excluded from the family circle. Unconsciously, but perhaps rather hurtfully.

'Please say what you can. As to Jane, she's devoted to Maud. They're very close, both emotional and headstrong. I'd never repeat anything that might harm or distress Jane.'

'The records that interested me, and Sir Hugh, consisted largely of documents concerning court cases that had made headlines during the post-war period of British administration in Nyangreela. And, of course, information about King Solomon.'

'What did you get on the King? I'm told he's a real autocrat, but astute, and trusted by his own people and neighbouring states.'

'His dossier is exemplary,' said Kim. 'A fine war record as a very young soldier still in his teens. And afterwards an impressive report from Cambridge, where he graduated before returning to Africa to succeed his father as Paramount Chief. Since independence he's proved to be a sensible and popular king. But these are difficult times in Africa where terrorism and assassination are endemic. The old cults ride again, Lady Etheridge.'

Mabel seldom smoked, but now she accepted the cigarette Kim offered her and inhaled deeply.

'Witchcraft, you mean?'

'Would it surprise you?'

'Nothing in this continent surprises me. The so-called motor-accident murders of churchmen and their wives; the gunning down of nuns in mission-schools and hospitals; the mass herding of school children across bush borders to enter terrorist training-camps instead of doing their normal lessons. . . .' She shrugged her shoulders helplessly.

'The Marxist terror-camp is the modern parallel of the traditional circumcision rites. It signifies the attainment of full manhood,' said Kim. 'No boy is a man today until he's learned to capture or kill cold-bloodedly – not animals but people.'

'Oh, yes, I see that. And, of course, trapping people is more interesting. Animals can't be made to talk, not even under torture.'

Kim gave her a thoughtful glance. 'Never go to an animal research centre. It isn't only human tongues that talk. A dog's eyes – a whimper. . . . However, don't let's be side-tracked. There were two crimes the British Administration in Nyangreela found impossible to eradicate. One was stock-theft – '

'There'll always be cattle rustling in cattle-country.' She smiled. 'I go to the movies and enjoy westerns on T.V.'

'Fair enough. The second was *diretlo* – medicine-murder. The British legal system in the dependencies imposed the death penalty for that. Chiefs, headmen and witches were strung up when they were found guilty, but the severity of the sentence proved no deterrent. In fact, in summing up a certain case in which the victim had been murdered and mutilated to provide . . . medicine . . . to strengthen a weak young chief, the judge had said: "However reprehensible civilised people may think this action, the fact is that it was done in order to do good to the chief and thus to the whole area. The murderers' intentions – from their point of view – were not malicious." '

Mabel shuddered. 'Yet he had to impose the full penalty?'

'In this instance the Witch-doctor and his confederates took the rap. Evidence which was very hard to get because no one would say anything proved that the young chief had wanted no part in the affair. In fact, he'd protested at the idea, but had been over-persuaded, almost forced, into the ritual by the Witch-doctor. The lad hadn't personally harmed the victim, but he'd partaken of the *muti* – the medicine – '

'And the mumbo-jumbo. Did it do him any good? Did it improve his image – to use today's jargon?'

'Everybody thought so. A whole village was involved. They had that all-important but nebulous factor on their side – faith. The crops flourished and later the chief turned out well!'

Mabel shook her head. Then she stubbed out her cigarette and turned to Kim.

'Who was the victim?'

He met her eyes frankly. 'The victim was an old White woman-farmer who lived alone and loved the country and its people. She was so successful in making her own land productive and breeding good cattle that she was highly respected throughout the area.'

'Who has the power of selecting the victim?'

'The Witch-doctor.'

She sighed. 'Thank God our doctors don't commit murder to strengthen a privileged patient!'

Kim answered slowly.

'I wonder if it isn't all just a question of interpretation? I used that comparison of yours to Abelard Cain and he was scathing. He said: "Your doctors just keep a dead person breathing artificially so that they can cut out his living heart and force it to beat in the breast of some sick human being. They cut out his kidneys too, if they're sound and somebody needs a donor. And his eyes? They put them in an eye-bank, so the poor devil returns to his ancestors mutilated and unrecognisable. He can't even boast the honour of being donor to a king or a chief whose life and health may be vital to a whole nation. He's just part of another experiment in human organ transplantation. And all this in a world the White scientists say is overcrowded!"'

'You'd make a good barrister,' said Mabel. 'But if a whole village was involved, and deliberately silent, how did the police find out what had happened?'

'It's curious, but in *diretlo* murders, a couple of decades ago, anyway, everybody needs to know what has really happened.'

'On the principle of "Justice must not only be done, it must be seen to be done"?'

'Precisely. That's why the victim's body was always left in some place where it would certainly be discovered and the word passed around.'

'Including the police?'

'Exactly.'

'But how could they get evidence from a mute community?'

'Because they knew the district, its people and its problems. If one person could be persuaded to drop a hint, the beans were spilt. Anyway, that's no longer our affair, thank goodness!'

'Perhaps *diretlo* is out of date. A symbolic sacrifice – a goat or cow – could have taken its place.'

'Possibly.'

She shivered as she rose and pulled on her wrap. He jumped up to help her.

'You've given me a lot to think about, Kim – some of it very frightening. But thank you for your confidence. I'm going in now.'

'Yes,' he said. 'I'll follow you soon. The wind's beginning to blow cold.'

'. . . thank you for your confidence.' Mabel had said it as if she'd been long excluded from the sharing of confidences. Yet this morning Jane and her stepmother had gone to the early service together as if they both felt the same need of divine support in this time of stress. They'd taken communion – the bread and wine, the 'body and blood' – to 'strengthen' them, and they had returned calmer, spiritually fortified. It's how you look at it, he thought. You twitch the cord of the venetian-blind just a little to alter the angle of the slats and the strong outside light enters the room differently. But it's the same light that is filtered.

As he sauntered up to the house Jane ran to meet him.

'Oh, Kim, I watched them go till I couldn't see the plane any more. This scheme should work, shouldn't it? It must!'

'In the circumstances I'm sure it will. Your father has the authority. Abelard is clearly acting on instructions. It's my bet that young man has a fat Swiss account of his own just in case the day comes when the African cauldron boils over. As for Des, he's as bright as a button.'

'But there'll be delays. They'll need Gran's signature.'

'To sign your mess of pottage away? Don't worry. Mrs Carpenter will co-operate. After all, she suggested this solution, knowing you'd want it. And when she's restored to her writing-desk she'll settle down and give us all the whale of a tale straight from her own experience, and it'll be filmed and televised and the shekels'll come pouring in to fill the ransom-gap!'

She tucked her arm through his. 'You're a comfort, Kim. Somehow, I've been full of misgivings all day. Just when it looks as if we'll really get her back. Silly, isn't it?'

He gave her arm a little squeeze as they went up the terrace steps.

'I'll get you a gin and tonic, and a Scotch for me. Elias has put the drinks trolley out to tempt us. Now, sit down, Janie, and try to tell me what's bothering you. What particular thing?'

'It's Gran's letter. Daddy said it didn't ring quite true. He was right. It's inconsistent that she should co-operate with the kidnappers to pay the full ransom. It's contrary to her own principles – her Creed, if you like.'

'Clause Five.' He set her gin and tonic beside her. '"Kidnapping," and I quote, "should be discouraged by the refusal of those blackmailed to pay ransom." Unquote.'

'What's more, Gran added that the *captives* should refuse to be . . . "objects of extortion".'

'Only if those captives considered themselves expendable. Mercifully, you've convinced her that she is not expendable. Her handwriting was even more forceful than in her first letter. So she's obviously being reasonably treated.'

'I've thought about that,' she said. 'Luckily Gran's extremely healthy. She's over sixty but she hasn't even got rheumatism and never takes a sleeping-pill. So I didn't expect her to crumble easily. But all these weeks, I've tried and failed to visualise her surroundings and her prison. Sometimes I've had nightmares imagining her in some sort of solitary confinement with cruel gaolers. And the chief kidnapper, the leader of the gang, if it is a gang, what sort of human being is he? I can't get the picture, Kim.'

'And now Abelard appears on the scene to effect your grandmother's capitulation. So where does he fit in? Leopard-Men and Abelard – savagery and sophistication in the same picture-frame.'

'All that. Lots of questions and no answers.'

Kim, sprawling in the rattan armchair usually occupied by the Ambassador, leaned down and patted Kirsty who had followed them onto the terrace and now lay peacefully between them. She twitched and whimpered as if half waking from her own doggy dream.

'Kirsty could give you as many convincing answers as I can. But I honestly believe that if Abelard is mixed up in this business – as he certainly is – Mrs Carpenter will not be ill-treated in any way.'

'You like him, don't you?'

'How can one help it? He has such gusto and he's excellent company. But I'm not stupid enough to imagine that I can really tune in to his mind. His thinking apparatus probably operates quite differently from yours and mine. It's a matter of upbringing and environment. His standards are not necessarily ours. He's a foreigner, Janie. To get right under his skin and into his brain might be to enter a labyrinth. Blocks and surprises all the way, and some pretty weird booby-traps to discourage intruders.'

'You're like Gran. You enjoy analysing people.'

'It's simpler than that. We both just enjoy people. They're a wonderful study if you accept them as they are. Analysis is something else again. It is detached breakdown by a neutral force. Or so I imagine.'

'Well, accepting Gran as she is, how do you see this . . . inconsistency in her attitude?'

'Look at it her way. To use a well-worn cliché, circumstances alter cases. That Creed was just a blue-print for general use – sensible behaviour in a world of violence and ever-increasing over-population. But it could well be that she now feels she has something more – and important – to contribute, and she wants to get out and be free to say her piece. Or again, she could just be bored with the monotony of her existence in whatever form her imprisonment may be.'

'Especially if they won't give her pen and paper so that she can keep one of the journals that are part of her writing equipment.'

'They'd never allow that. She'd only be given the chance to write messages at the command of her Captor –'

'That Captor? Commander, Captain, King –'

'Jane!' Kim broke in. '*King*! Could it be? No, it's impossible. . . .'

Jane stared at him wide-eyed.

'Is it? I wonder. She knew him when he was Paramount Chief.'

'How did she come to know him?'

'In the late nineteen-fifties my grandparents were staying with the Governor. King Solomon had recently succeeded his father as Paramount Chief. Gran and the Big Chief got on like a house on fire. She admired him enormously. She told me not long ago that he was a highly enlightened traditionalist, determined to preserve old tribal customs while moving with the times. But she wondered if he could maintain his absolute autocracy in today's world.'

'The old and the new can survive in an African stew-pot,' said Kim. 'Leopard-Men and Harvard-trained bright lads like Abelard.'

'If this unknown Captor were the King, she would be well-treated,' said Jane confidently. As Kim did not answer, she pressed the point. 'Don't you agree?'

The need for reassurance was now in her voice and in the dark eyes that searched his face so hopefully.

'Of course, Janie. But we mustn't pin our hopes that high. Kings are more often kidnapped than kidnappers. We've no real reason for thinking King Solomon is involved. Just intuition. . . .'

'You're not with me any more,' she said as he lapsed into silence. 'Where are your thoughts, Kim?'

He rose and touched the soft silkiness of her hair. The gesture was more tender than he knew. But his mind had retreated into the Embassy Library.

'I'm with you,' he said, 'and with Maud Carpenter and the phantom figure of an African king.'

While the Ambassador and Yates were in Geneva Mabel Etheridge organised her share of the Embassy move from Cape Town to Pretoria.

Kim, meanwhile, was ahead of them. He had flown to Johannesburg on Monday in time to keep a lunch date with Abelard in Judy's penthouse.

Abelard was in high spirits. He looked round in approval.

'Nice little pad this and your . . . mmm . . . source has laid on a cold lunch for two and a bottle of wine in the fridge. What do you know!'

'Not enough.' Kim's tone was chilly and Abelard raised his eyebrows. 'We're here to talk in private. Since you're in on the Maud Carpenter snatch, I want to be sure of one thing.'

Abelard studied the pink gin in his hand and moved the glass so that the crushed ice was prismatic in the sun slanting through the open window.

'What is that one thing?'

'When the financial deal is concluded and the transfer safely in the kidnapper's bag, can we be one hundred per cent certain that Maud Carpenter will be returned to her family?'

'Of course,' said Abelard.

'And if there's any unexpected hitch in the deal?'

'There'd better be no hitch, unexpected or otherwise. I can't make any promises for my principal if things go wrong.'

'H.E. and Desmond will be in Geneva this afternoon, and you tomorrow morning. We're doing our best not to involve Nyangreela in any way here, and the same will apply in Geneva, as far as journalistic snoopers are concerned.'

'I'll see that any get-togethers are kept secret,' Abelard agreed. 'I'm not exactly a new boy in this school you know.'

'I know. And I'm counting on you to be sure that when I splash my story it will have a happy ending.'

Abelard raised his glass.

'Here's to the happy ending.'

On Tuesday night the Ambassador put through a call to his wife on a private line from the luxurious lake-side home of his host, Baron Hans Weber. Yates was with him.

'Speak freely, Hugh,' Weber had said. 'Nobody will tap this line. I'll leave you to it.'

'Mabel?'

'Yes, Hugh. I'm here and Jane's with me.'

'Good. I have splendid news! Thanks to the influence of my host, all problems have been swept aside. Abelard is already on his way home with the documents to be signed by Maud. He should be back here on Thursday evening.'

Jane, watching her stepmother, saw her relieved expression reflect the elation in her father's voice, and her own heart lifted. She was perched on the edge of the study desk right by the telephone, ears strained to hear his end of the conversation, while Mabel sat in his swivel chair and Kirsty lay on the rug in front of the empty grate.

'That's wonderful,' said Mabel. 'So when can we expect you back?'

'Des and I will remain here till the documents are signed and the whole transaction is properly wrapped up. That should make Friday night possible. Or Saturday at the latest. When exactly do you go to Pretoria?'

'Tomorrow by the noon flight. Elias and the staff are there already, except Salima. She's looking after us and she'll fly up with Jane and me.'

'Well done. I hope it hasn't been too tiresome – all the last minute things that had to be arranged?'

'No, Jane has helped me. Everybody has done their bit. In fact, we've been thankful to have our hands full.'

'Put Jane on the line, darling. I want a word with her.'

'Goodnight then, dear Hugh, and you'll ring us at the Embassy in Pretoria tomorrow night. I know there won't be any news by then, but we'll want to hear from you. Take care of yourself and get some rest in the next couple of days. Here's Jane.' Mabel passed Jane the receiver.

She was breathless with excitement as she took it. 'Daddy, I caught most of what you said! It's wonderful – '

'I hope it will be. When everything is satisfactorily concluded we'll have a marvellous family reunion in Pretoria. Des wants to speak to you. He has my permission to do so.' Jane heard the smile in her father's voice. 'So over to him . . .'

'Janie! The world's a wonderful place today – '

'I know! It's all too thrilling to be true!'

'Listen, Janie, there's something else that's thrilling! I told your father this evening that I wanted to marry you – '

'Des! Why on earth . . . ? Is Daddy still with you right now?'

'He's very tactfully handed me the telephone with a gracious wave of his hand and vanished through the French doors.'

'But, darling, why talk to Daddy about us? People don't bother with that sort of stuff these days. I'm twenty-one!'

'So you are. But, Janie, I work with H.E. and in some ways I think I know him better than you do. What's more, I admire him tremendously. I just wanted him to realise that my intentions are matrimonial.'

'I'm not sure mine are.'

'If only you were here in this glorious city I'd make you sure. There's snow on the Alps and spring in the air, and, when all this suspense and anxiety is truly ended, we'll come here for our honeymoon.'

'You're crazy,' she laughed shakily. 'And I love you. But we've a lot to talk about. Marriage isn't something we can rush into – '

'Ssh . . . your father gave me all that – and a lot more too – half an hour ago. All I care about is that I miss you and want you, and, if you feel the same way, it's mad not to be together every second we can for the rest of our lives.'

When she finally set the receiver in its cradle she did so gently, as if it held something brittle and precious. She felt weak and light-headed, tears glistened on her lashes and when she looked up Mabel was no longer in the room.

'Your father gave me all that – and a lot more – ' Des had said. Yes, Daddy will have told him everything, she thought. He has too much integrity to leave Des in the dark.

She knelt by the dog on the hearth rug and patted the rough coat as she said softly:

'I'd never spay you, Kirsty, without allowing you one litter first. Just one! So I shouldn't blame my mother, should I?'

And now it's Des and me. No money and no babies but he still wants me. I believe him and from the way he talked I'm sure he knows everything and doesn't care. Whatever we go without, we'll have each other. Gran will be glad for me. She took my 'personal problem' so much to heart with her resentment of Ann's attitude and her fears for me because one day I'd find myself up against the same decision. In a way she tried to make it for me in Clause One of her Creed – the unselfish way – a sacrifice to safeguard future generations. What'll we do, Des and I? Already I'm looking for loopholes – the right to give another life to this rotten, evil, miraculously lovely old world.

13
'This is a big deal. Winner takes all.'

Kim was at the bookstall on Wednesday morning when the passengers from the Swissair flight came through the International barrier into the main hall of Jan Smuts.

Abelard paused to buy a paper and hesitated before he chose a Carpenter paperback thriller. He unzipped his canvas overnight bag and Kim inadvertently jostled his elbow so that the book slipped to the floor.

'Sorry,' he said. 'Clumsy of me.'

He picked up the paperback and returned it to Abelard.

The Nyangreelan nodded, smiled and went his way to the special hangar area where his own private helicopter awaited him.

Kim went into the coffee lounge and ordered a black coffee while he buried himself behind a paper and opened the brief note that had been pressed into his hand.

> Everything set. Only signature required. Hope to make the daylight flight from J. S. tomorrow.

Kim waited to watch a helicopter rise steeply into the fierce blue of the sky above the highveld. Where would it land? Among the mountains of Nyangreela, or on the green bank of the Big River? The mountains probably, or Abelard would have taken his Cessna. If so, it could be risky flying after sundown when the mists often settled on the peaks at this time of year. Or was Mr August Obito expert enough for flying blind? Kim decided that he probably was. He looked at his watch. Nearly noon. He'd go along to the Southern Sun and ask Judy out to lunch. She'd been very co-operative about Abelard. About Jane too. Ah, Jane, better not to think about that one.

It was mid-afternoon when Abelard touched down in a perfect landing on a small granite plateau some half-hour's horseback ride from King Solomon's upland kraal.

This landing-pad was isolated, a natural altar created by the ancient tribal gods for important ancestral rites. Wild creatures used it for their salt-lick and humans for rituals which were never mentioned once their purpose had been fulfilled. Above and around the bare sacrificial-rock the forests loomed, marking the winter snowline. A grassy arena surrounded it, and below it a torrent cascaded from the high Nyangreelan watershed on its serpentine route to the Big River and the fertile plain below.

A perilous stony path followed the course of the ravine which was broken here and there by waterfalls plunging into deep calm pools fringed with ferns and orchids.

As Abelard alighted from the chopper he found himself singing for the sheer joy of life, anticipation of seeing his girl, and pride in bringing off the preliminary part of an important deal and, he hoped, planning an equally important rescue.

He looked around expectantly.

A tall figure on a pale horse moved out of the forest fringe into the afternoon sun. He was clad in his Witch-doctor's white mantle and baboon-fur turban and adorned with all his traditional trappings.

He was closely followed by a young groom leading three horses, one piebald for the Director of Nyangreelan Intelligence, one black sturdy animal for himself and a pack-horse.

Without further ado the groom tethered his beasts to the branch of a tree and then secured the rotor-blades of the helicopter.

Samuel Santekul remained mounted as Abelard joined him. He looked down at his nephew with approval.

'Welcome, kinsman!'

As the young man bowed his head in greeting Dr Santekul lightly touched the black frizz, recently straightened by the French hair-stylist at Hydro-Casino, but crinkled now by the sharp breath of the mountain breeze.

'It seems you have done well. Is everything in order? Are the documents properly drafted? This is a big deal. Winner takes all.'

Abelard laughed. 'You'll be satisfied, Uncle. Nothing is needed except the hostage's signature properly witnessed.'

A slight frown furrowed the Witch-doctor's forehead.

'The King's captive is cunning and obstinate. I don't trust her.'

'Does she trust you?'

Santekul's hatchet-thin face relaxed into a half smile at the impudence of the young man's implication.

'We must be on our way,' he said. 'You must take off again before nightfall.'

'So you don't trust the weather either or my ability as a night-pilot?'

'Your success – so far – has gone to your head. You were always cheeky even at Solinje's age.'

'Ah, Solinje! He's a child after my own heart.'

'And after the captive's. She loves Solinje.'

'And he?'

'He loves her too. There is something that binds them together – a cord as powerful as kinship.'

The little procession set off in single file along the narrow stony path above the mountain-torrent. Santekul took the lead, then

Abelard, with the pack-horse next, and the groom's black pony in the rear. The pack-horse required no leading-rein, he simply followed the piebald ahead of him, encouraged now and again by the crack of the groom's long *sjambok* which scarcely flicked his broad rump. The animals were all sure-footed Basuto ponies, well accustomed to mountain-tracks, and wherever the path widened or flattened they broke into the familiar quick triple characteristic of their breed.

'Wait!' called Santekul suddenly. 'My horse whinnies, the wind wails, the water chuckles and further down the path a woman sings, sweet as birdsong at daybreak.'

He drew his pale mount into a grassy bay at the roadside and waved his nephew on.

'Go ahead, Abelard, and meet the singer!'

Abelard spurred the piebald with urgent heels. As he rounded a bend he saw Dawn on the path leading to the kraal, a load of firewood balanced on her wide swathed turban. He reined in his horse so that he might watch and enjoy her grace. One arm was raised to steady her burden, her broad glossy thighs and sturdy calves moved easily under the brief woven kilt. Her back was towards him but he knew how softly her bead necklaces would lie between her jutting naked breasts. She would bear him many children, not like her sister, who, after Solinje's birth, had made herself barren with the White women's pills. No wife of his would ever be allowed to do such unnatural things!

Dawn stopped and turned her head carefully as the clatter of hooves was resumed and her lover waved a greeting. Her fluted song ended in a trill of rapture and she raised her head to return his salute, careful not to disturb the balance of her load.

Abelard caught his breath at the grace of her poise and balance, her shining face and great soft eyes. Where, in Geneva, could a man see such beauty?

He read the bead-messages in the cleft he could hardly wait to caress. He swung his leg across his horse's neck and threw the reins to the groom who had come up behind him.

Dr Santekul and the groom bowed to Dawn as they approached the young couple and continued on their way to the kraal. She called a greeting after them and Abelard waited impatiently for them to round the next bend. Then he clapped his hands happily and took the burden of fire-wood from her head. He set it on the ground while he embraced her.

At last she whispered in their own language:

'I heard the throb of your Big Bird and saw it come down to alight on the Sacrificial Rock. I told the other stick-gatherers to hurry down to warn the King that soon you would be with him. We knew the River-doctor was waiting for you at the Rock, and King Sol was already here at the kraal. He came at noon on his golden horse. There is great excitement here today.'

'So there should be! But our time together is too short, Dawn. I must fly back to Jo'burg tonight to make an International connection tomorrow.'

'International?' Her eyes widened. 'Where to?'

'I must not say. In any case, much depends on the outcome of the next few hours, which reminds me.'

Abelard drew a paperback out of the capacious pocket of his safari-suit.

'This is a present for you. See, it is one of Maud Carpenter's thrillers.'

'How wonderful!' she exclaimed. 'I'll ask her to sign it for me.'

'Do that! Right away when you get back. *Before I see her.* I want to study that signature. Okay?'

'Okay. And thank you. But now we must move on! Lift my bundle onto my head. It's time to go.'

Here, where it was necessary to walk in single file, it was the custom for the woman to carry the burden and the man to precede and protect her, his *knopkierie* or hunting-knife ready to hand.

'How is Mrs Carpenter?' Abelard asked over his shoulder as they followed the trail once more. He had never met Maud Carpenter and he was curious about her. He had seen films and plays of her books, and the press photographs and he knew that in the kraal they called her 'the Wise One', a high honour.

'She is well in body,' said Dawn, her voice troubled. 'But since Dr Santekul chopped off her hair she has drawn her head into its shell like a tortoise. She no longer talks to me as she used to. Even Solinje can't interest her when he tries to teach her to make music with a reed-pipe. It is as if her mind, inside the tortoise-shell, is seeking a quiet place to commune with her own ancestors. But she has not yet turned her face to the wall.'

'Why should she? She has only to write her signature on some papers and then she can feel sure that the ransom money will be paid to King Sol – the price of her freedom. That should please her.'

Dawn made no reply and Abelard shouted impatiently.

'Don't you agree?'

The trail had begun to widen and she came up with him so that now they could walk abreast.

'She is born of our African earth, and, as a child, she lived in a tribal land. Such children have an understanding of our people and our customs. The Wise One has never lost it. That day, when your kinsman from the Big River sliced off her braids, she knew that now he held her in his power.'

For a moment Abelard's bland face looked unhappy. Then it brightened as a boy rushed to meet them, a dog bounding at his heels.

Abelard ran towards Solinje who sprang into his outstretched arms while the dog yapped joyously round their legs, demanding attention. The very old and the very young spilt noisily through the thorn-fence to crowd round Abelard, but, as they entered the kraal, Dawn saw that Mrs Carpenter was not among the people, nor was she sitting in the sun outside her hut. Dawn remembered that she had not even come out earlier in the day when King Sol had arrived.

'Where is the Wise One?' she asked Solinje.

The boy's eyes were clouded as he looked up at her and Abelard.

'She is in her hut,' he said. 'She, who loved people and sun, now likes to be alone in the shadows.'

Across the threadbare grass of the compound they could see Dr Santekul talking to the Rain-Maker. Abelard had always instinctively disliked the Rain-Maker, but he knew better than to get on the wrong side of a sorceress, so he never failed to exert his charm for her benefit.

'There comes your father, the King, with your mother, the Little Queen,' he said to the boy. 'We must join them at once. Today I am the bearer of good news and as such I am a welcome person!'

Dawn entered Mrs Carpenter's hut and stood for a few moments, eyes narrowed against the shafts of late afternoon sunlight slanting through the tiny square window onto the silhouette of the figure sitting in the *riempie* armchair. Mrs Carpenter's head was bowed in thought so profound that she seemed unaware of the girl's form in the doorway.

Even now, with plaits shorn, the fair-silver hair made a halo in the gloom. Dawn repressed an impulse to stroke it. She moved lightly to the table and placed a gourd upon it. Mrs Carpenter's eyes opened wide at the rosy fruit it held and a dreamy pleasure filled them.

'"Comfort me with apples . . ."' she quoted.

'No,' said Dawn. 'This fruit is not from an apple-tree.'

'Of course not, my dear. It's straight from an "orchard of pomegranates". Maybe the missionaries don't teach their pupils King Solomon's "Song of Songs". It's very melodious and very erotic – a pastoral love lyric.'

Dawn said, 'These . . . pomegranates . . . don't taste as good as they look. But they are pretty so I thought you'd like them. They grow on trees near the stream.'

'You've even put them on a paper doily!'

The girl smiled. 'The mission teachers show the children in playschool how to cut out doilies.'

'So you thought you'd cheer me up? Well, you have. More than you can guess. Thank you, my dear.'

Dawn sat down opposite Mrs Carpenter.

'Will you do something for me, please?'

'Naturally – if I can.'

'See, my boy-friend has given me a present.' She drew the Maud Carpenter paperback from the cloth-bag in her hand. 'It would make me very happy if you signed it.'

'Good heavens! A fan at world's end! I'd love to sign it, but our King Solomon does the writing here and refuses to let me have a pen or paper unless I write at his dictation.'

'I have a pen.' She dipped into her bag again. 'Here it is.'

Mrs Carpenter held the commonplace ballpoint as if it was purest gold.

'I've forgotten how to sign my name,' she smiled. 'This'll be good practice.'

She turned to the title page.

'Here we are. "*Maud Carpenter. The Vixen*". I'll sign it across my printed name.'

She scrawled the words Maud Carpenter in the bold slanted signature well known to her fans. She added a message. 'Inscribed for

Dawn with gratitude and affection. World's End.'

'Thank you,' said the girl, smiling. 'You are very kind, Wise One. But why do you put "World's End"?'

'It's my address at present and, up here in the mountains, it's halfway to heaven.'

Dawn shook her head as Mrs Carpenter proffered the pen.

'Keep it, please. You will need it soon. My boy-friend has brought papers for you to sign. The King and the herbalist from the Big River, Dr Santekul, will come with him to see you and to witness your signature.'

'You have given me fruit and a pen, and now I ask for yet another present.'

'Tell me what it is you want.'

'More than anything I want a little flat bead-bag such as you sometimes wear on a long string of beads. Perhaps one day I shall be in a position to give it to my grand-daughter. It would mean as much to her as it would to me.'

'I will bring you mine,' said Dawn. 'Later, when I bring your food. But tonight please eat what comes from the Little Queen's stew-pot. You have not been out lately so you are no longer hungry, and that is bad.'

When Dawn had gone Mrs Carpenter swathed her turban about her head. She had grown quite good at that, so, when she looked in the hand-mirror the Little Queen had given her, she saw that her head was stately but her face was gaunt and her skin no longer supple. It was taut over the fine bones, sallow as sandalwood. Autumnal, she thought.

She hid the ballpoint in the pocket of her cowhide mantle, and she took the doily. She folded it carefully and put it with the pen.

Then she prepared to receive her guests.

They stood there, forming a semi-circle before her as she sat at the table, the stapled papers under her hand with the spaces at the bottom of each page blankly awaiting her signature and those of the witnesses to the hieroglyph that could take a fortune from the person she loved most. Jane.

It wasn't too late to change her mind. On the other hand, she thought with a bitter little grimace, it means a sacrifice either way.

Five people watched her intently. The King, in a formal suit, his hand on the bare shoulder of his son adorned with beads, bangles, a loin-cloth and sheepskin anklets; Abelard, towering over Dawn at his side, and – slightly apart from the others – the Witch-doctor with his axe-thin face, skeletal hands and all the bizarre trappings of his official status. Geometric white designs masked his face.

Thank goodness they've left the Rain-Maker outside, thought Mrs Carpenter. There really wouldn't be room for all that blubber in my hut. I'm claustrophobic enough as it is!

The felt-pen she held poised over the paper had been provided by Abelard. She didn't care for it. She preferred her hidden ball-point. She raked her small audience with a resentful glare.

'I don't like doing this,' she said, as if it were not yet too late to refuse.

Abelard was nervous. He had been put in charge of this part of the deal. He forced a grin.

'Oh, come now, Mrs Carpenter. You're not signing your death warrant. Far from it!'

Her eyes met his without amusement and passed over Dawn's head to the King, whose expression was sullen with some inner disapproval. She glanced briefly at Samuel Santekul whose make-up she detested – the mirthless fearsome clown – and her gaze rested on Solinje and focused finally on the little strawberry birth-mark over his heart.

'My death warrant was signed by fate,' she said. 'Some seven years ago.'

The well-folded turban dipped as she bent her head and laid her left hand on the paper to control it. For a moment the felt-pen was poised as if about to dive into deep waters, and then the firm flowing signature Dawn had already seen in her Maud Carpenter book embellished the document in heavy black ink.

Mrs Carpenter rose to allow Abelard and Dawn to witness it. Then, with a slight obeisance, acknowledged by King Sol, and a nod to the rest of the company, she turned away in a gesture of dismissal.

The hut seemed lighter when she was alone and the level light flowed uninterrupted through the inadequate doorway.

Yet she was not quite alone after all. For once Solinje's dog had not immediately followed at his master's heels. She felt his wet tongue sweep her right hand and she looked down at him with a sudden smile of contentment.

'Dog,' she said. 'Thank you for the blessing.'

14
'Motives can be strange and improbable.'

Baron Hans Weber was a stocky middle-aged financier, fresh-faced and cheerful company in spite of a world recession, which, owing to his foresight, was unlikely to compromise his personal fortune very seriously. He was a widower with a teenage son at Gordonstoun, a daughter studying art in Florence, and a flock of dazzling young and pseudo-young women eager to share his bed and help him reduce his vast fortune.

He liked entertaining congenial house-guests but refused to join them for an English breakfast, a meal which he considered barbarous. He read the morning papers and studied the financial columns uninterrupted over a light continental *petit déjeuner* on the balcony outside his bedroom. Woods and the snow-capped Alps were reflected in this corner of the lake and the air was stinging-sweet with the aphrodisiac scents and sounds of late spring on the threshold of summer.

When he joined Sir Hugh and Yates on the patio he had news for them.

'Your intermediary, Mr Cain, returned late last night. I've just had a telephone call from him. He's coming here from his hotel before we go to the bank.'

Sir Hugh, fit and rested after a few days of relaxation and Alpine air, said:

'That's quick work. Left here Tuesday night, back Thursday night! Did he get Maud's signature?'

'He said Maud signed on the dotted line – without much enthusiasm – and he was one of the two witnesses to that signature.'

'Is he happy about it?' asked Yates.

'He sounded jubilant.'

Sir Hugh's voice was dubious as he said:

'I'd like to check that signature before we go to the bank.'

'Of course. I have specimens of Maud's signature in my library precisely for that purpose. Forgeries are possible and there's a great deal at stake in this case.'

'Especially in her outlandish circumstances! There's another thing, Hans. That Creed of hers – the one I showed you – keeps nagging at me. There's an inconsistency somewhere. You know how inflexible she is where her principles are concerned.'

'You mean that Clause Five – "hostages should refuse to be used as objects of extortion" or something like that?'

'Frankly, yes.'

'My dear chap, it's easy enough to propound such a theory, but when it has to be put into effect, very few normal healthy people – and that includes Maud – would feel inclined to make a quite unnecessary self-imposed exit just as a gesture. Maud's much more likely to cling to life so that she can write a first-hand account of being snatched by Leopard-Men and kept in captivity by . . . ?'

The Baron broke off and used his well-manicured hands to signify a bewildered query. Desmond filled in the ensuing pause.

'That's the trouble, sir. We can't picture the where and the who, much less the conditions under which Mrs Carpenter is being detained. Naturally we are pretty sure the *where* is Nyangreela and the *who* someone fairly powerful and outside politics. But there speculation loses its way.'

'We've no reason to think she's being ill-treated,' added Sir Hugh, 'and physically I imagine she's all right because there's been no request for pills or prescriptions of any sort. Mentally there can't be much wrong either. Her last letter to me was clear and exact and her writing normal. However, you've seen all that for yourself.'

'Perhaps our mediator can enlighten us further now that he's made contact with both his so-called principal and the hostage. Ah, there's the doorbell! Surprise, surprise! Our Black clients seldom show any respect for the clock or one's time. They buy our splendid Swiss watches – only the most expensive – and use them as ornaments. By disposition they prefer the garden sundial. Let us go to the library.'

The library, into which the Maltese butler showed Abelard, was spacious, lofty, and well furnished with tables and chairs for the use of any scholar wishing to spread out the material he happened to be studying. High Gothic windows looked out upon the green garden view of a croquet-lawn surrounded by trees and shrubs in full leaf and flower.

The rows of shelves held Abelard's attention while he waited for his host. Lavishly bound rare volumes lined one wall, books of reference another, modern fiction shared a third with historical, scientific and biographical material. Periodicals of every variety were neatly spread on an antique mahogany table and the big leather-covered desk was bare except for writing-materials. A magnificent Turkish carpet covered the polished floor.

Abelard's glance swept this quiet room with its evidence of a mind covering a wide spectrum of interest and activity and he thought that one day he would like just such a room for himself – somewhere to learn and reflect and get away from the clamour of the large family Dawn would surely give him.

He turned from admiring books in French, German, Italian and English as Baron Weber entered with Sir Hugh Etheridge and

Desmond Yates. His pulses quickened in anticipation of reaching an immediate conclusion of the big deal that would later yield a handsome profit for his own services and an even higher one for his uncle, Samuel Santekul.

'You look as if you'd had a pleasant flight, Mr Cain,' smiled the Baron. 'And I hope a successful mission.'

Abelard greeted the three men and then opened his brief-case with a flourish.

'The papers,' he said triumphantly. 'Signed and witnessed. The hostage, you will all be glad to know, is in good health and looks forward to an early reunion with her family.'

Sir Hugh's grey gaze fixed the young emissary with a more than usually glassy stare.

'Did *she* say that? Or do you?'

For a moment Abelard was disconcerted. The hostage had said remarkably little and made no mention of her health or her family. The Baron cut in before he could stammer out a reply.

'Now then, Mr Cain. Let's waste no more time. Please pass me the documents.'

He seated himself behind the desk, waved to the three chairs in front of it and stretched out a hand for the papers Abelard had taken from his brief-case.

Sir Hugh, who seldom smoked before the evening, lit a Havana and drew on it deeply. Yates helped himself to a cigarette and offered one to Abelard which was refused.

Baron Weber studied the documents with a faint frown. Abelard felt a touch of apprehension. There couldn't be anything wrong? It was impossible. The Baron unlocked a drawer in the desk and drew out a file. He opened it and after a few moments looked up.

'You witnessed this signature, yourself, Mr Cain. You actually saw Maud Carpenter write it.'

'Of course. We all did. Five people.'

'And you are sure Mrs Carpenter was in her right mind? In no way under duress?'

'Never! It was she who had devised this plan, in any case. His Excellency knows that. So does Mr Yates.'

Abelard sprang up and went to the shelf containing modern detective and spy fiction. He had noticed that a collection of Maud Carpenter's first editions had pride of place. He drew one out at random and turned to the title page.

'There!' He placed it on the desk and the bold inscription leapt out at them, slanting across the printed name of the author. Maud Carpenter. 'It's the same, you see! Like the ransom demands. There can be no mistake.' His voice had risen.

Baron Weber ran his hands over the broad dome of his forehead and smoothed his sparse hair. His shrewd blue eyes took in the surprise on Yates's face and the sudden apprehension gathering in Abelard's expression, dispelling his proud excitement.

'What's wrong?' the Nyangreelan asked at last. His anxious gaze flickered from one to another of his companions and came to rest on the Ambassador's face which, in the last few minutes, had aged as if some fatal half-expected blow had suddenly struck him.

'Tell him, Hugh,' said the Baron. 'You are an executor in Maud's will and you know her wishes. Her Creed and her ransom notes – partly dictated, but conveying their own underlying meaning to you personally – must have prepared you for something of this sort. You, of all people, must realise the dilemma which faces us now.'

Sir Hugh balanced his Havana carefully on the ashtray slot and the pale smoke filtered upwards in the still air of the library. The signature in the open novel seemed to hypnotise him. He cleared his throat before speaking.

'When that last ransom demand came with this Swiss proposition from Maud, I knew, somehow, that it didn't ring true. I said so at the time, as Desmond can tell you. But I couldn't see the catch. Now I believe I do.'

He turned slowly to face Desmond, whose clear green eyes were wide with enquiry.

'All this complex game has been played out to test *you*, Desmond. It was to test the extent and sincerity of your love for Jane. You passed the test with honours.'

Abelard, who had remained standing, leaned forward with furious impatience.

'Baron Weber, I have put before you a very important document, properly signed by the hostage herself, and duly witnessed. Now what does it become? A mockery! A love-test! This is frivolous and fantastic, and I must ask for a reasonable explanation. We are here to conclude an extremely serious transaction. If it is not expedited the hostage will be killed. We are not considering the quality of love but a matter of life or death.'

As his anger exploded over them like a thunderclap, Yates knew that Abelard was right. A life hung in the balance. Jane would eagerly have given her heritage to save Maud Carpenter and Desmond loved her the more for her loyalty. But what about that Creed? Was Maud really just proving *herself*?

The Baron agreed with Abelard that this was no time for sentiment. This was a grave predicament for everyone concerned. He addressed himself directly to the Nyangreelan.

'Mr Cain,' he said. 'I am sorry to tell you and His Excellency and Mr Yates that we are quite unable to accept this signature, whether Maud Carpenter wrote it or not. I believe she did write it and that her purpose in doing so was deliberate, whatever that elusive purpose may have been.'

He indicated the open file which lay beside the document

Abelard had put on the desk.

'Here are several specimen signatures signed by Mrs Carpenter over a period of years. These photostats speak for themselves.'

He turned the file towards them. There it was. 'Maud Jane Carpenter.'

The three words were run into each other and the effect was quite dissimilar to the simple two-name signature which Maud Carpenter used for her private correspondence or fan-mail.

Baron Weber continued:

'It is impossible for us to carry out instructions not validated by the only authentic signature we recognise as Maud Jane Carpenter's. Public figures, who are constantly asked for autographs, usually protect themselves in this way. We prefer that they should do so. I realise that this must come as a great shock to all of you here this morning. Perhaps, as Sir Hugh suggests, Mrs Carpenter had her own reasons for putting us all to a great deal of useless trouble. At present I can only tell you that there can be no transfer. It is a case of "as you were".'

He added to Abelard:

'I only hope, Mr Cain, that you can persuade your principal to restore Maud Carpenter to her family as soon as possible, and regard the attempt at extortion and blackmail as abortive. If so, there will be no attempt at any follow-up from our side. The matter will be closed.'

•

Kim and Jane were playing singles when Mabel Etheridge strolled over to the tennis-court that same afternoon. They smiled and called to her to fetch her racquet, but she said, 'Don't stop. I just want to watch and relax.'

In fact, she felt anything but relaxed. Numb, was more like it, and totally unwilling to tell Jane news that could only upset her. Let her dart about the court and try to outsmart Kim. At least the two young opponents were demonstrating physical activity and enjoyment. Soon enough they'd be back in the chasm of suspense. Here, on the heights of Bryntireon where beautiful homes stood in well-tended gardens, Mabel tried in vain to conjure up the scene of Maud Carpenter's incarceration and the mental state of the captive. It couldn't be done. Just as well, perhaps! She forced herself to concentrate on the players.

Jane was quick about the court, all dancing feet, long legs and muscles flexed, racquet striking the ball early and accurately, dark head shining in the late afternoon sun that fell so softly on the blue hills curved about Pretoria. But, agile as she might be, Jane was no match for Kim. His speed, reach and powerful net-play as he smashed or volleyed, made an end of any opening she happened to give him.

He's dark lightning, thought Mabel. If I were Jane's age, ah, but I'm not, and that too is just as well, maybe!

'Game, set and match,' said Jane as they joined Mabel. 'I give in. Even using a borrowed racquet and giving me a fifteen–love start on my service, Kim's got me on toast.'

Mabel rose and put a cardigan about her stepdaughter's shoulders.

'It's getting chilly. Have you two had enough?'

'I couldn't play another stroke and I'm dying of thirst,' said Jane, sinking into a chair.

'Lemon and barley?' asked Kim.

She nodded.

'And for you, Lady Etheridge?'

'The same.'

He filled their glasses from a jug of home-made lemon and barley water and poured a light ale for himself. Then his shrewd glance took in Mabel's expression. At once he was alert, invisible antennae quivering at the scent of news.

'You're holding out on us, I do believe! You've heard from Geneva?'

She looked at him, her eyes sombre. As she turned to Jane she saw the young face, flushed with exertion, sharpen into quick anxiety.

'Has Daddy 'phoned, Mabel?'

'Yes. Just before I came out here. It seems there's been some hitch.'

'Please tell us everything the Ambassador said.'

Kim sat down beside her. His deep voice and his presence calmed her. She recounted her husband's description of the morning's meeting in the Baron's library. It had been, as usual, exact and perceptive.

Mabel said: 'I asked Hugh if he thought Maud could have written her fan signature in error. Surely it could have been some sort of nervous mistake. She's so used to autographing books for people that possibly, just for an instant, she lost her head, and, out of habit, simply signed automatically.'

Jane began to protest but Kim shook his head slightly as if warning her to keep quiet.

Mabel continued.

'Hugh was most emphatic that it was no mistake. He said that such a slip could only have occurred if she'd been drugged. Then he explained logically and patiently that the very last thing the kidnappers would want would be a muzzy signature – one that might appear to be written under pressure. After all, Maud had put up the idea herself and then. . . .' She sighed helplessly. 'It turned out to be a pricked balloon.'

'Go on,' Kim prompted.

'Hugh thinks Maud either foxed them deliberately, perhaps to gain time, or for purely personal reasons of her own. Curious motives are, after all, her stock-in-trade.'

'It could be simpler,' suggested Kim. 'She might have changed her mind at the last minute and decided to reverse the exercise.'

'So what now?' Jane's voice was low.

'Your father and Desmond are taking tomorrow's day flight. They're to be met at Jan Smuts. In less than twenty-four hours from now they should be with us here.'

'And Abelard?' asked Kim.

Mabel's usually smooth brow creased. 'Hugh says Abelard was genuinely shocked and astonished at the turn of events. It seems he is now trying desperately to get on a flight from Switzerland tonight. My husband and Des return tomorrow afternoon.'

She rose, shivering visibly.

'The moment the sun sets the temperature drops. Let's go in. By the way, Kim, you must be on standby here for a call from Geneva about nine tonight. In the meantime not a word to the media. There's still a chance of Abelard persuading his principal to re-negotiate. It's the only hope.'

The call was brief and unsatisfactory. The Ambassador had a word with his wife and daughter but his business was with Kim.

'Abelard's frantic and not too good at concealing it. He can't get a flight earlier than ours tomorrow and the moment he arrives in Johannesburg he'll take his chopper onto . . . goodness knows where! Will you be sure it's serviced and ready for him?'

'Of course, sir. But can't he get in touch with his principal before that? By telephone or telex?'

'He refuses to try. Of course he's afraid of a clue that could be followed up by Interpol. More even than that, he's terrified that if the kidnapper knows for sure that the hostage is being deliberately unco-operative he will carry out his threat without further negotiation.'

'Then we must accept Abelard's judgment. He's the only one

among us who knows the characters he's dealing with.'

'But we do know the hostage. And it could well be that she'll refuse to co-operate over the ransom payment.'

'If she does, the outcome looks bad.'

'Our flight from Geneva is due to arrive tomorrow afternoon. Desmond has the details. I'll turn him over to you now.'

Desmond spoke to Kim and then to Jane. When she put down the receiver she was pale.

'He tried to sound hopeful,' she said.

'We have to hope, Janie.' Mabel put her arm round the girl's thin waist. 'Surely the kidnappers will wait to see Abelard. A million is a lot of money. They'd never throw the bulk away out of pique or impatience. After all, the motive is surely personal greed.'

She turned to Kim, her eyes pleading for reassurance.

'It would appear so,' he said. 'But *is* the motive for this snatch pure greed? If it is, we'll get Mrs Carpenter safely back.'

'We know the motive isn't political. What else other than greed could it be?'

Jane's questioning look sought reassurance from Kim. He forced a smile of encouragement as he said:

'What indeed, Janie?'

But Mabel recalled her conversation with him by the swimming-pool in the lee of Devil's Peak.

Now he said quietly:

'Motives can be strange and improbable. Let's hope this one is as mean and simple as it seems on the face of it. Greed. And a greedy person will bargain till the last hope of gain has gone. It's up to us to keep that last hope alive.'

15
'... beyond the dark curtain between day and the long night.'

Since writing her last letter to Hugh Etheridge and signing that phoney signature Mrs Carpenter had behaved in the classic manner of a person under an African spell.

She had turned her face to the wall.

It was well understood in the kraal. Yet the Little Queen was worried. About the time that Kim was taking the Ambassador's call from Geneva, the Little Queen was in bed with King Sol. Their pillow-talk was serious that night.

'If the money for you is to be paid into a Swiss numbered account, as she must expect, why is she not pleased? She must surely believe that she will receive her freedom when the deal is settled.'

'She is not called the Wise One for nothing,' said Sol, who had been in a bad mood since the signing. 'When Santekul lopped off her plaits she knew what it meant. She had been chosen.'

'That was some time ago. She didn't turn her face to the wall then.'

'She began to change. It was then she knew that it wasn't a question of "your money or your life" any more. It was a statement. "Your money *and* your life!"'

'When do you expect Santekul and his men?'

'When the half-moon climbs above the horizon.'

'In an hour's time.'

'A little more. Let's not waste it.'

'Again . . . ?' she laughed.

'I am not yet a hundred years old!'

Solinje had left his parents' hut earlier. Like most children, he found it rather frightening when his father and mother 'fought'. His father always won. It was right that a man should be top-dog, especially a king, but he preferred not to witness his mother's defeat.

Across the compound Mrs Carpenter had let her hut-fire die right down even though, here in the mountains, the autumn nights were already sharp with frost. In winter the peaks would be snow-crested and the kraal deserted.

She lay on her divan, face to the wall, covered by her jet-blanket and jackal-skin kaross. She was curiously indifferent to the cold penetrating her bone-marrow. It was, to her, another stage in a protracted act of renunciation, a farewell to life with, she told herself, 'a proper acceptance of whatever may lie beyond the dark curtain between day and the long night.'

She was not afraid, but odd flimsy thoughts meandered through her mind, forming and dissolving inconsequentially.

Her limbs were numb and the nape of her neck was frozen without the mane of thick hair that had once fallen to her waist.

'Samson,' she muttered. 'That powerful buffoon must have felt like this when Delilah betrayed the secret of his strength and had him shorn of his locks. What a fool he was! The biggest braggart in the Bible, spoilt by his mother, besotted with his treacherous wife – all brawn, no brain, a certain amount of yokel cunning, a freak. . . .'

She pulled her blanket higher over her shoulders and tucked up her knees as if to compress her body into a knot of concentrated human warmth. But, even in this foetal position, she felt embalmed in ice.

She did not turn when she heard the hut-door open and light familiar footsteps patter across the baked-mud floor. A child and a dog. At this time of night? Surely not! It had been dark for a long while. It must be after nine o'clock when the old and the young slept and dreamed and the cattle were quiet in the byre unless the barking of dogs gave warning of a marauder.

Solinje's dog whimpered and pawed at her back and the boy said:

'Why do you lie that way, Wise One? All tucked up.'

His voice came from somewhere near the shorn back of her head and she knew that he must be squatting on the floor very close to her with his leopard cape warm around his small body.

'I am returning to the womb,' she answered, and found herself amused. That'll shake him! she thought. The dog had jumped onto the divan and lay across her icy feet.

'The . . . woohm?' Solinje repeated. 'I don't know that thing.'

'Let us say, then, to the time and place before I breathed the air of this green earth, and knew the seasons and the joy of life and love and what it means to have a man and bear a child . . . and lose them both.' Her voice trailed into the shadow of sorrow.

He pondered a while. The manner in which she spoke – turned away from him as if she addressed someone else – was beyond his comprehension, yet his own acute instinct endowed her words with meaning.

'I understand,' he said after a while. 'But the time is not yet. It is too soon.'

'Too soon for what?'

'To return to your ancestors.'

The dog had crept up and was near her face. His breath was on her neck and in her nostrils.

'Dog,' she complained. 'You've been eating buck again, and

high at that!'

He uttered a thin brief whine of apology, breathed heavily into her face and washed it with his friendly tongue.

'Oh, Lord!' groaned Mrs Carpenter. 'The kiss of life!'

She turned with a surprisingly quick uncoiling movement, and saw the crouching motionless figure of Solinje silhouetted against the patina of stars in the Madonna-blue sky outside the tiny window.

She rested her chilly hand on the round warm head with the neat close-fitting ears characteristic of his people and felt it lift in quick response, like the playful butting of a lamb. He jumped up and fetched her long cowhide mantle from the shelf on which it lay and wrapped it round her shoulders. She sat up and drew the kaross across her knees and the dog quickly curled up in the hollow her body had left.

'How on earth do you come to be here now, Solinje? The kraal sleeps.'

'My father, the King, is fighting with my mother. After the battle they sleep. It is always so.'

She smiled. He was still a child, for all his precocious pre-knowledge.

'You have never come to me before like this.'

'Tonight we heard you call us – my dog and I.'

'What will happen when your mother wakes to find you gone?'

'She will think I am with Dawn and she will go back to sleep.'

'Have you been with Dawn?'

'Yes. She gave me this for you.' He opened the leopard-skin pouch he wore across his shoulder and took out a bead chain with a small flat bag attached to it. 'Dawn said to me, "I too hear the Wise One call you. Go to her, Solinje. Tell her I wish her well in all things."'

Mrs Carpenter looked at the little bead-bag in wonder.

'It's most beautiful! No present could please me more. You are the messenger tonight. Give Dawn my thanks.'

'When she brings your food tomorrow you will be able to thank her yourself.'

'I think not, Solinje. Tonight I must talk to my ancestors and to our descendants. They are all about me.'

'I know. You wish to be alone with them.' He stood up, his head on a level with hers as she sat on the bed beside the dog who twitched and sighed in some dream hunting adventure. 'But before I leave I must breathe new life into your fire.'

'Do so then, Keeper-of-the-Flame!'

Her voice had grown in strength as they had talked and she spread her fingers wide towards the heat of the dry autumn sticks and cow-dung flaring up on their bed of ash. She heard the crackle and saw the red, blue and gold growing like hot grass in the central hollow of the mud-floor.

'There! That is better.'

Solinje wiped his hands and called to his dog.

'Your dog has warmed my bed,' said Mrs Carpenter. 'And you have warmed my hut and my heart. Go well, Solinje.'

'Stay well,' he replied in the language of his country.

When the door had opened and closed once more she felt in the pocket of her mantle and found the paper doily that had lined Dawn's calabash of pomegranates and the ballpoint pen with which she had signed the paperback.

She would write to Jane and fold the letter into the little bead pouch.

It would have to be a short letter. No matter, she had a strong premonition that her time too was short.

When King Sol entered Mrs Carpenter's hut an hour later the gibbous moon was just showing above the horizon. The night was one of extreme beauty, silvery and windless, silent but for the sounds of nocturnal creatures and the murmur of the torrent thirsty for the autumn rains.

He was surprised at the sight of her. She was not lying with her face to the wall, as he had feared and expected. On the contrary, she was clad in ceremonial attire, and, at his knock, she had opened the low door and had bent the knee to him in so doing. Her features, recently honed down to angular sharpness, now seemed smoothly serene, almost impish in the firelight. Her short hair, brushed and gleaming, was no longer concealed by an austere turban but ornamented by a broad bead-fringed forehead-band from hairline to eyebrows. As well as her deep bead bib she wore a long necklace with a flat purse which hung like a locket over her heart. She had swathed her jet-blanket sari-fashion round her body, and her cowhide mantle lay across her divan ready to cover her from shoulder to ankle. She was dressed proudly for an occasion.

He stood amazed. She smiled.

'Even sheepskin socks,' she pointed out. 'More elegant than the usual woolly operation stockings. Wouldn't you agree?'

She touched one of the *riempie* armchairs.

'Please sit down, King Sol. Then I can do the same. Is Solinje bringing us a loving-cup of maize beer?'

'Would you like that?'

'Very much.'

'I will call Solinje.' He went to the doorway, put his little-fingers in the corners of his mouth and uttered a shrill whistle.

'That should wake the dead!' she remarked.

When he had shouted his orders to his son he returned and sat down, plugging his carved pipe with the tobacco that left an agreeable aroma in the reed thatch. He was wearing his bead-kilt and leopard-skin cape and, when he bent to light and draw on the pipe she knew so well, she observed the flamingo feathers dartlike in the thick greying mop of his hair.

'What goes on tonight?' she asked. 'The kraal is deserted. A little while ago there was a commotion as if the people were all going away.'

'They were going to the Ritual Rock,' he said. 'The time has come for the Rain-Maker to conduct the rites that will ensure good crops in the plain below.'

'Where is this rock you talk about?'

'Higher up the peak, along the track above the torrent.'

'And the sacrifice?'

'The goat.'

'The goat? He is rather a friend of mine. I'll be sorry to lose his company. He was usually tethered near my hut.'

'You won't lose his company, Mrs Carpenter.'

Outside, in the quiet of the near empty kraal, a rousing bugle-call announced the arrival of Solinje with the calabash of beer.

The boy crouched between them as usual when he had offered the 'loving-cup' to his father and the Wise One and had enjoyed his share of the brew with them. Mrs Carpenter noticed that he, like the King, had the flamingo feathers of the royal clan in his hair. It was the first time she had seen him wear them.

'Surely you will be present at the ceremony tonight?' she said to the King.

'Of course. And you too.'

'Is it far to walk?'

'You will be carried by my royal chair-bearers. The trail is steep and rough, but the chair is rattan, light and comfortable. Two poles are fitted to the arms, and four bearers, one at each corner, shoulder these poles and hoof it steadily and safely up the rise.'

'I see. And you, King Sol?'

'I will ride my golden horse with my son sharing my saddle. The groom will follow on his black pony.'

'I shall be in good company. When do we go?'

'Soon. The people will be assembled by now. The moon is rising and at midnight she will reach the zenith of her course. It is then that the sacrifice must be made.'

'After that the clouds will gather?'

'Tomorrow there will be thunder and lightning. Towards evening the first rains will bless the land.'

He passed the calabash once more; then he said to Solinje:

'Go now! Tell my chair-bearers to be ready, and the groom to bring the golden horse. Then wait outside this hut with them till the Wise One and I are ready to join you.'

The boy dashed off to do as he was told, but King Sol appeared in no hurry to move.

'Tell me,' he said at last. 'Why do you love Solinje?'

'That is simple, King Sol. He is a manly child with a happy disposition and great intelligence.'

'That could be said of many of my sons, and other children too.'

'But this one does not think only with his quick brain. He thinks with his heart also.'

'You have noticed that?'

'I've had good reason to. I am not of his family or his nation, yet he reads my mind as if I were his own grandmother, and when it is sick he comforts me. It was very sick this evening.'

'You had turned your face to the wall?'

'The chill of death was in my bones when Solinje came to me with his dog. He said they had heard me call them. He said: "The time is not yet to return to your ancestors." He gave me life and courage. Only one other person could have done that for me.'

'Who, Mrs Carpenter?'

'My grand-daughter, Jane Etheridge.'

'Abelard has told me she is a fine young woman.'

He opened his leopard-skin pouch and replaced the pipe which he had tapped out over the embers and allowed to cool. As he withdrew his hand he was holding some sort of weed and a small phial containing opaque liquid.

'Do you know this plant?' he asked.

Mrs Carpenter took it from him and examined it with interest.

'It's like a large specimen of English hedge-parsley,' she said at last. 'But the stalk is different – rather sinister, so smooth and spotted with purple. Where did you find it?'

'It grows near the Big River in the Herbalist's garden.'

'Indeed!' She raised her eyebrows. 'Then what does it cure? Or kill?'

'It makes an interesting tisane,' he said. 'Or a small effective potion. It has many uses.'

She gave him a long searching look which wandered to the phial he held up for her inspection. To him it seemed that she read his mind. Suddenly the old familiar sparkle lit her face with the half-hidden amusement she so often employed in an effort to reduce the horrific to the ludicrous.

'Wait!' she cried. 'I believe you are offering me a pre-med, King Sol. A very potent one.'

He accepted her attitude with relief and allowed a smile to warm his voice. 'We don't call you Wise One for nothing.'

'It's strange,' she said. 'All my novelist's life I've played God to my puppets, made them dance to my tune, killed them off without a care – victims or predators – and strewn their corpses by the hundred in unlikely places, yet never once have I seriously considered death itself, its profound spiritual implications. It was just a card in my conjuror's pack or a piece in a puzzle. Now I begin to wonder! Am I afraid? . . . No, not of death itself, only of the manner of my dying. So I thank you, my friend, for this precious gift.'

She stuck the little plant in her headband.

'By the way, what is it?' she asked.

'Hemlock.'

'The poison used by the Ancient Greeks for those condemned to death. Socrates was given his dose for telling his students that their sexy, quarrelsome, amusing Olympians weren't the real thing. The true God was one divine spirit of eternal life.'

'And he was still telling them that when at last he fell asleep.'

'So it takes some time to do its work? What did Keats say in his "Ode to a Nightingale"? "My heart aches, and a drowsy numbness pains my sense, as though of hemlock I had drunk, or emptied some dull opiate to the drains one minute past, and Lethe-wards had sunk. . . ." '

'I'm told it doesn't taste too bad. The Herbalist is clever at disguising nasty medicine.'

'Is he a good surgeon as well as a good druggist and physician?'

'He is a hunter. Like all hunters he is dextrous with the knife.'

'But he operates without an anaesthetic. If an organ – the heart perhaps – must be removed from a donor, that donor must be alive when it is taken. Am I right?'

King Sol found himself shivering in spite of the warmth in the hut. His discomfiture made him irritable with his victim who had turned interrogator, putting her finger on the tender points he wanted to dismiss from his consciousness.

'People are always undergoing surgery they dislike and fear,' he said sternly. 'I've given you the only real help I can. Take it in one gulp when you know the inevitable is about to happen.'

'Before Santekul can bind my hands or tape my lips.'

'Enough! Aah. . . .' He cried out as if he himself were suffering intolerable pain. Part of him knew that he too was Santekul's victim – bound by the ancient cults. Unwilling, yet subject to ancestral hypnotism.

She rose steadily and her eyes under the bead fringe were compassionate.

'King Sol, you are trapped between two worlds – the old and the new. You are breaking the old rules out of kindness to me. I am grateful for this hemlock and I shall use it sensibly. There is one other favour I crave. If this necklace I am wearing, with the bead-embroidered purse like a locket, could find its way into the hands of my grand-daughter, Jane Etheridge, I would reckon the account between us well and truly balanced. There has been some cheating between us on both sides. This gift from beyond the dark curtain to the person I love most could settle the score and my ghost could never haunt you. It would only strengthen you. I hope that Solinje's generation will grow in pride and enlightenment.'

He led her out into the fresh fragrant mountain air. Near her hut he mounted his golden horse and one of the bearers swung Solinje up onto the saddle in front of him. Followed by the groom on his black pony, they moved out through the thorn-fence, the dog ahead of them. Mrs Carpenter took her place in the rattan chair.

As the four bronze bearers lifted the poles her sense of occasion deserted her. She clasped the little phial tightly between her cold hands. King Sol would have paid a high price for this hemlock. For a moment she closed her eyes and let the last recorded words of the Greek philosopher echo in the dim recesses of her conscious mind. 'Death is recovery from the fever of life.' How could he be sure? she wondered. Soon she would know. Meanwhile she could hope that Socrates was right. The leathery feet of the bearers jogged rhythmically along the winding uphill trail and when she opened her eyes once more she saw, between the thinning autumn branches, the silver purity of the moon nearing its zenith between rising and setting.

16
'...The moon was high. The drums were beating...'

Mabel, Jane and Kim met the Ambassador, Desmond and Abelard at Jan Smuts International Airport soon after three o'clock on Saturday afternoon.

The travellers looked worried and weary and Abelard was clearly anxious not to waste a moment before continuing on his journey.

'There's nothing really to be said,' he told Kim, 'till I've had a chance to confer with the Captor. Meanwhile, for heaven's sake, keep the press out of it till you hear from me! Is the chopper ready for take-off?'

'Yes. I may manage to see you before you go. If not, get in touch with me tonight at Judy's flat.'

'I will,' promised Abelard.

'He was so bucked when he produced the signature,' said Desmond to Jane 'What a triumph turned disaster!'

'For all of us,' Jane said. 'Incidentally, I drove your car here from Pretoria, so you and I can go back on our own.'

'Good work!' He smiled his relief. 'Now let's get your father and Lady Etheridge on their way. It's not been easy for H.E. since that phoney signature blew all our hopes to blazes. We had a bumpy flight and he needs rest.'

Kim and the Ambassador arrived at a satisfactory understanding promptly.

'Are you coming back to the Embassy with us now, Kim?'

'With your approval, sir, I'd rather stay here. I want to find out what sort of news is likely to break – and where. Your flight and Abelard's movements have been connected by the bright boys. I've got to hold wild rumours in check.'

'How?'

'I don't know. One gets an instinct about it. I might even take a flight on my own to Hydro-Casino. If so, my source, Judy, will know and she'll contact Jane at once. In any case, sir, be sure that I'll be in constant touch with you one way or another.'

'I must rely on your discretion entirely. In fact, I do. We'll keep in touch.'

It had been given out that Sir Hugh's visit abroad had been to London to attend to personal affairs. So, at Mabel's request, even the British Minister had refrained from meeting his Chief at the airport.

As soon as Yates had seen Sir Hugh and Lady Etheridge off in the official Embassy limousine, he and Jane set off in his Mercedes Sports.

'Janie, love,' he said, once they were on the Main Pretoria Road, 'there's nothing more we can do about your grandmother till we hear from Abelard or Kim. So let's just get the you and me situation clear! Will you make me the happiest man in the world and marry me just as soon as is reasonably possible?'

'Darling, I love you. I want you. But how much has Daddy told you?'

'Just about everything, I should think. I know that if the re-negotiation succeeds and Mrs Carpenter will sign her bank signature, you'll inevitably lose your inheritance. That doesn't matter a fig to me. I can support you even if not in the manner to which you've been accustomed. I know about the other thing that could come between us. It won't. There's no reason why it should. But your father insists that it is *his* right and responsibility to tell you the whole truth. He's brave and chivalrous and I respect his attitude. That's why I felt he ought to realise that I was serious about you. I wanted him to know it when we all reckoned your inheritance was Mrs Carpenter's life-price. Anyway, he'll talk to you tonight when he's rested. He's been under terrible strain.'

She was deeply touched and for a time they were silent as they sped along the broad freeway to the capital.

'Very well then, Des,' she said at last. 'Just tell me one more thing. Did you let Daddy guess we were lovers already?'

He answered slowly and not at once.

'No, Janie, I did not. That was never the way *I* wanted it. It was your wish. Oh, God, I wanted you, as I do now, for better, for worse and all the rest of it. Not just as another temporary girlfriend. But you shied away from the very thought of marriage. I didn't want your father to think that living together sporadically and no strings attached was good enough for me. It wasn't and it isn't. When you've talked to him I shall ask you for a real answer and no more evasions.'

He turned the Mercedes up the hill towards the Embassy and she saw that his profile was stern and set.

'You really mean that, Des?'

'With my mind, heart and body. Either you tell me I'm your man now and for keeps, and a gold band on your finger to proclaim as much, or I'll walk right out of the picture. And, if my jealous instincts are right that'll be the signal for Kim to walk right in. He's not the marrying kind and maybe that'll suit you better.'

About an hour later Abelard made his usual perfect landing on the Ancestral Rock in the rosy hour before sunset.

He saw it all before his feet touched the stained granite and a cold horror shook him, though he had half expected this aftermath of a celebration.

Traces of a recent fire were contained in various horn-shaped semi-circles of heavy stones at the far end of the altar slab. A few bones lay among ash still warm from the barbecue of the night before and the day's sun. The grass round the edge of the rock had been trampled by many feet where old and young had danced and feasted. There were bloodstains everywhere, and as Abelard walked slowly to and fro across the sacrificial area he saw the fragments of hide, hair, hoof and bone, but not what he most dreaded to find.

Many must have come from the Big River, he thought, especially for the rain-making ceremony, and they would have brought a beast – probably a cow selected by Santekul, but naturally not from his own opulent herd. And here was surely the ear of the goat from the mountain-kraal which must have turned on the spit above the smaller wire grid, its cynical golden eyes plucked out to stew in the heavy iron cauldron of the Rain-Maker.

There was one more surface to explore, a small arm of level rock. While the big beer-drink was going on elsewhere it might possibly have served as a side-altar, hidden from the singing and the dancing.

He entered that secluded corner reluctantly, treading softly as if on hallowed ground.

There were ashes here too in the shape of the Rain-Maker's tripod. Blood had been spilt. Stuck to its stain was a jewelled scattering of beads from the elaborate bib he had observed Maud Carpenter wearing on the day she had signed her false signature.

The young man swept the yellow beret from his head and knelt on one knee with bowed head. He tossed the beads into the beret with his right hand and wrapped them carefully before plunging them into the pocket of his anorak.

'So now you know what has happened.'

The thin reedy voice of the Witch-doctor brought him to his

feet with a shock.

Santekul's bony features were still accentuated by geometric white markings. The grass-snake, coiled about his throat, shone as if enámelled by the level rays of the sun. Abelard knew the snake to be harmless, the emblem of ancient Greek healers, but every rippling movement of the creature or the flickering forked tongue made his blood run cold.

'I don't understand,' he said hoarsely. 'You were to wait for my okay! This was only to happen if I reported failure. I have not done that.'

'When last we met, nephew, I said "Winner takes all".'

'I heard you, but I refused to believe it of our King.'

Santekul raised his head and the snake did likewise. The fur of his baboon-skin turban trembled in a faint breeze as he said:

'I had a vision when you flew back to Geneva. I saw you in a high spacious room of books containing the wisdom of many lands and years. You showed the hostage's signature to a man with a well-fed paunch and thinning hair, pale as my own pale horse. He refused to honour it because the hostage had written two names instead of three on the deed of transfer. You sprang to your feet with a cry. I *heard* that cry.'

'Very well then. You saw and heard these things that were going on in Geneva, so far away, but surely it was your duty to wait for me and allow me to continue with the bargaining.'

'We can still do that. Winner can still take all.'

Abelard drew in his breath with a long hissing sound.

'I wash my hands of it. I do not bargain for the life of a dead woman! Is the King here at the mountain-kraal?'

'The King and Solinje are in my house by the Big River. Everyone has left the mountain-kraal. The beasts too. The Rain-Maker has gone to the River. Only Dawn is still at the kraal.'

'Why is she there?'

'I told her you would come today.'

'How did you know?'

'Because I have the seeing eye as you understand.'

'Will you lend me your horse to go there and fetch her?'

'If you wish.'

They found the pale horse hobbled, cropping sweet grass contentedly. The black pony was near him.

'Take both animals. The black follows like a shadow.'

'Is your groom here?'

'I am alone. I will wait for you. But don't be too long. Soon the thunder will begin to mutter above these peaks.'

The kraal was indeed deserted. The huts were closed, the byre empty, no fowls pecking in the footworn grass, no tethered goat to butt maliciously at Solinje's dog. No cries and laughter of children at play, no cook-pots simmering and chatter of women, or cackle of old men smoking their pipes and taking a pinch of snuff.

Only Dawn and the wild birds brought life to the empty scene within the thorn-stockade. She ran towards the sound of hooves but stood away, hands over her mouth, as she saw the pale horse on which Abelard rode, the black pony behind him. He tethered both animals to a pole and held out his arms to her. He felt the strength and springy softness of her body against his own.

When they had watered the horses they went into her hut to fetch her suitcase.

'I am to go with Dr Santekul to his house by the Big River. That is why he kept the black pony. For me to ride. King Sol's car will meet us lower down the road where it is broader.'

'You will not go with him,' announced Abelard. 'You will come with me in my chopper to Hydro-Casino and there we will be married.'

'Santekul will be angry. My sister too perhaps.' She looked alarmed but there was a new strength in him.

'Even the King will not stop us. We will marry properly. I will give your father the *lobola* – whatever bride-price he demands, for you will be my only wife. I shall want no other. Never.'

Her eyes laughed. 'That is not the custom of our people.'

'It will be. Many of the customs of our people will change. After today you will wear your hair in the beehive style of a married woman and cover your breasts with a sari. But not yet, my love.'

He made her his in the deserted kraal, on the straw pallet which was her sleeping-place under the reed thatch, and when she uttered her small gasp of pain and ecstasy and left a trace of blood on the pallet, he felt the full pride of possession and the deep tenderness of a man who has initiated his mate into the total acceptance of her womanhood.

Afterwards, when they were nearing the Ritual Rock, she spoke to him of the Wise One.

'It happened after the rain-making rites, when the people began to dance and sing and the drums throbbed. Then it was her turn and the crowd did not know of it. Or, if they did, Santekul warned them off.'

'So what then?'

'It was very strange. She did not struggle or cry out, not even when Santekul and the Rain-Maker laid her on the hard flat rock. Nor did she protest when the Rain-Maker tore off the beaded bib. But she asked that the King be given my long bead necklace with the little pouch. So this was done . . .'

'And then?'

'She lay quite still, as if she slept. The King said, "Let her sleep!" So, when her eyes closed and her hands fell limp, Santekul did what he had to do. Solinje buried his face against my body but afterwards, when he saw her so peaceful and pale, he was comforted.'

'So later . . .?'

'There was the *muti* – the medicine in the Rain-Maker's cook-pot – and it was inhaled by those of us who were there. The King, Solinje, the Little Queen, Santekul, the Rain-Maker . . . and me. The King and Solinje partook of the sacrifice that they might be enriched by her wisdom and by her thinking heart.'

'After that?'

'I don't know. She was borne into the woods on a litter. The moon was high. The drums were beating, there was singing and dancing and King Sol commanded us to join in the feasting of those who had roasted the ox and the goat.'

'Then, at first light, everybody went their way and those at the King's kraal did the same?'

'Yes, Abelard. As you have seen. Stop now! There is Dr Santekul coming to meet us.'

The Witch-doctor helped Dawn off the black pony and took the reins of his own pale horse.

As he did so an ominous rumble of thunder rolled among the mountains and a flash of lightning followed. Santekul said with satisfaction:

'The rains will break tonight. The storm is on the way. You must hurry, Abelard! Dawn and I must go now before rain falls and the path grows slippery and treacherous.'

The sun had set, but the sky was still fiery with its glory of red and gold. Abelard looked at it and thought how good it would be when the rain fell upon the Ancestral Rock and washed it clean of last night's happenings. He felt very strong now that he had possessed his woman and was her lover and her master. He was strong enough to cross swords with a sorcerer as dangerous as Samuel Santekul.

'Dawn will not go with you, my uncle,' he said. 'She will go with me to Hydro-Casino, to the house of her parents.'

He took her light suitcase and climbed up to put it in the helicopter. When he turned to the Witch-doctor again he was surprised to encounter no resistance.

'Dawn must do as she wishes,' said Santekul.

'I will go with Abelard,' she said. 'He is my man.'

'Go soon, then. The storm strengthens. Go well.'

He watched them enter the helicopter and saw it take off into the threatening sky.

Thunder muttered and he tightened the rein on his horse as it reared with flaying hoofs at the first flash of lightning.

'Go well!' he repeated. 'You know too much, my kinsman. And your girl was too fond of the Wise One. It is best that she share your chariot of fire in this stormy twilight.'

17
'Life here is close to nature and so, perhaps, to revelations.'

'Hugh,' said Mabel when the Ambassador had given her and Jane a résumé of the Geneva fiasco over a late cup of tea. 'You must relax. I hate to say so, but you look done in. Where is Des?'

'Typing and annotating the facts as far as they go. There's really nothing any of us can do till we hear from Abelard.'

'Do you trust him?' asked Jane.

'Oddly enough, yes. In any case, he's our only hope.'

The Ambassador made no move to take the hot bath and rest his wife had advised. Instead he dismissed her gently but firmly.

'I have to talk to Jane, Mabel. Alone. There are facts that should have been clarified between us a very long time ago. If you'll excuse us, we'll go to her sitting-room. It's nearly six now. Desmond will be coming to dinner at eight. No one else.'

'As you wish, my dear. I'll tell Elias to put your usual whisky and water in Jane's sitting-room, and gin and tonic and lemon. Then you can help yourselves when you want to.'

He smiled at her with gratitude. She was thoughtful for him but knew when to let him have his way without any fuss. There was nothing he detested more than being fussed over except flying, which he found insufferably boring.

He followed Jane upstairs and settled himself in a comfortable chair. He noted that her books and belongings had already impressed her personality on this pretty extension to her bedroom. The so-called sitting-room led onto a small enclosed balcony where clustering bougainvillaea cascaded over a wrought iron parapet.

On a small escritoire he saw the familiar photograph of Jane's mother in its white frame. So cruel that she should have died at the height of her beauty. Lung cancer. Perhaps, today, medical science could have saved her.

'She would have been so proud of you, Janie,' he said.

'I wonder, Daddy? I can't really remember her. We aren't very alike, are we?'

'You're more like Maud,' he said. 'But you have Ann's lovely turn of neck and head, her grace and sense of buoyant life. Meeting her there in Greece, one saw the pagan side of her. You have it too. She was a dryad, a spirit of the forest and the earth, elusive and erratic as spring itself.'

He paused, his tapering fingers holding the photograph as if to draw her magic out of the frame. The sunset, accentuated by the abundant pink, scarlet and magenta of the bougainvillaea, imbued his tired face with borrowed light and colour, and, for the first time, Jane saw him as Maud Carpenter had written of him over twenty years ago. ' . . . distinguished-looking in his austere way . . . fairish with most arresting grey eyes and really beautiful hands . . . sensitive on the reins of a horse . . . with a woman too, no doubt! Sportsman, gambler,' she'd added, and then, ' . . . yet there's something inhibited about him . . . obviously deeply in love with Ann. And she loves him too. But there's a difference.'

Jane took the journal from a locked drawer.

'There are markers in this, Daddy. I think you should read those marked passages alone. You'll see then that they came as a shock to me. A very great shock.'

He frowned.

'But what is this particular journal, Janie? One of Maud's many diaries? She always kept them like a Victorian. And how did you come by it?'

'It's not like a Victorian diary at all, you'll find. And I came by it the evening Colonel Storr told us she'd been kidnapped. She'd always told me *this* diary was for me. It was never to fall into other hands. The day she could no longer keep it herself I was to take it – *and then only* would I have the right to read it.'

He stared at her, disbelieving.

'So that's why you rushed upstairs. You meant to fetch and hide this journal from the police or anyone else?'

'Yes. If you'll read a bit further on, Daddy, when Gran and Grandfather came to stay with you at "The Ridge" some months before my mother died, you'll see that I learned only by accident why I have no real right to marriage or motherhood. Why didn't you tell me yourself? I love Desmond, but he deserves everything marriage has to offer. I dare not give him children. You knew that but you never told me. Did you tell Des in Geneva?'

He rose and helped himself to a whisky and water.

'I did *not* tell him that in Geneva because it isn't true. There was nothing I could tell him about you that could stunt your marriage. Money? Well, Maud's savings may or may not come to you. Des doesn't care. It's you he wants. Now, go out onto the balcony, or change in your bedroom and make yourself look presentable. Then come back to me here. Meanwhile I'll read what Maud discovered.'

She turned the pages to the entry about the visit to 'The Ridge'. She laid it open on his lap.

'There it all is. Read it and we'll discuss it when I've changed. There's not a word I don't know by heart. After all, you and my mother directed – or misdirected – the course of my future life. There are no easy decisions for me now.'

He watched her go through the connecting-door to her bedroom, and, then, with his customary thoroughness, he settled down to read.

When he finally closed the journal he knew that Maud Carpenter had received only half a confidence from Ann. He sighed deeply. He alone was to blame. He had meant to tell Jane everything himself, but two factors had held him back for too long. Love and loyalty.

As Jane came back into the sitting-room, showered and changed into a long printed skirt and plain scarlet blouse, she drew up a little footstool and sat at his feet. She had observed the sad exhaustion on his face and it had wiped her own clean of all reproach. Pity had taken its place. She preferred him not to notice that, so she rested the back of her head against his knee. He touched her hair gently, relieved that she could not read the record that must be reflected on his face – love, joy, frustration, bitter jealousy, and the secret battles he had fought against an unknown enemy – the lover of his wife and the father of the child he loved as deeply as if she were his own flesh and blood.

'It's all true, this journal, as far as it goes, Janie. But it doesn't go far enough. I ought to have told you everything long ago. If your grandmother had known she would have driven me to do so much sooner, but she was ignorant of the most important factor.'

'Tell me everything, then, Daddy. Don't torture yourself. Just give me my problem fair and square.'

'You have none, darling, because you are not an Etheridge, except in name and by virtue of the love I have always had for you. To me you have been my own child.'

'What?' She gasped and he held her shoulders tightly.

'When I met your mother she was a young secretary in the Embassy typing-pool. I fell in love with her. I knew that there could never be anyone else for me. She was just about to take her local leave, and she went to Crete. Alone. She was fascinated by the myths and legendary gods and goddesses of ancient Greece. She could speak the language. She only had a week in Crete, and she hired a mountain-guide to take her up into the wild savage country she longed to explore. They stayed a night in a shepherd's hut, or in a cave or wherever seemed a good camping place –'

'Gran might have done the same. So they fell in love?'

'Love is a big word to my way of thinking, Janie. What Ann wanted she took without a scruple. She never even knew his name except that he called himself Heracles and afterwards, just before they parted after that fairly brief affaire, he told her he had a wife and family. She laughed. The whole encounter was as impermanent to her as to him.'

He paused, and, after a while, Jane said faintly: 'So this Heracles was my father.'

'Soon after her return to Athens I asked her to marry me. I was really the one with the guilty secret. I told her that generations back in our lineage there had been two cases of Crouzon's Disease – a hereditary and tragic gene that might possibly recur. I told her that I had been sterilised so that this tragedy would end as I was the last of our line.'

Jane half turned.

'How did she take it, Daddy?'

'She told me that she was going to have a baby. She said: "I will never see the father of my child again. He is married with a family. He is superbly healthy and handsome and a fine mountaineer. But although we were happy together in a wild and beautiful setting I knew him for what he was – a brave, splendid peasant whose mind could never match or satisfy my own. As yours does, Hugh. And, if you can't make babies, I assume you can make love." She assured me then that it would not trouble her to have no more children. But this one – you, my Janie – she wanted beyond all things. And I craved fatherhood. We had a wonderful marriage. I believe only death could have broken it. As for you, you were all we needed to make it perfect.'

'But you didn't tell Des all this?'

'Why should I? That curse in my family could never touch either of you. If you want to tell him everything, do so. It's your right.'

'Perhaps one day we'll go to Crete and hunt for a rugged peasant called Heracles,' she said softly. 'But the man I shall always know as my father is right beside me now this instant.'

'Bless you, Janie.'

He raised his head as Mabel's step sounded on the landing.

'Come along, you two! It's high time we had a sociable drink before dinner. Des is waiting.'

Dr Santekul had looked at the luminous dial of his watch as Abelard's helicopter circled over the Sacrificial Rock. Half-past-six, and already the gathering rain-clouds were smothering the fierce glory of the sunset while the first flashes of seasonal evening lightning, followed by thunderclaps, echoed ominously among the peaks.

Dr Santekul could smell the coming rain. He did not fancy being caught in a deluge on the rocky track above the torrent, but he was anxious to see the result of his very modern experiment. Another minute and a half would tell him all he needed to know.

Directing the course of lightning by strategy plus will-power was hazardous, exhausting and frequently unsuccessful, whereas the planting of a neat little gadget like a small napalm time-bomb should be simple, accurate and foolproof. He had learned much from Californian psychiatrists while working at an American hospital and just recently he had found many interesting things he could barter for in the terrorist camps that abounded along every

African border. For instance he had exchanged the napalm bomb for a love potion, and, of course, instructions had gone with the deal both ways.

He examined his watch once more.

Fifty seconds to go.

Abelard's chopper was beginning the steep descent towards the forests that lay between the mountains and the lowveld of Hydro-Casino.

'Forty-eight,' counted Santekul, as lightning forked down off the iron rocks of the precipice, and on its heels came the mighty crash of thunder. The helicopter shuddered against the darkening sky like a long-tailed insect caught in a sudden gust of wind. For an instant it seemed to stand still in space. Then, as Samuel Santekul intoned the word 'fifty', it burst into flame. The sparks flew far and wide as the 'chariot of fire' exploded, its burning fragments scattering flaming torches into the forest and bush tinder-dry after the long hot summer.

The Witch-doctor saw with satisfaction the rapid spread of the funeral pyre. Yet he was moved too by regret. His nephew, Abelard, had been outsmarted by the trickery of the Wise One. In any case, that young man was moving too far from the ancestral cults and he knew too much of this Carpenter affair for anyone's good. As for Dawn, she had become attached to the Wise One. It was better and safer this way.

He mounted his pale horse, and he led the black pony down the trail to the deserted kraal. He would sleep there tonight and commune with the ancestral spirits of his nation.

He put the horses under shelter before he entered Dawn's hut, where he saw that the young lovers had indeed been united. He closed the door and crossed the compound to the hut of the Wise One. He stayed there for some time absorbing its atmosphere. He did not even stir when the grass-snake uncoiled itself from his neck and slithered towards a bowl on the baked-mud floor, its forked tongue flickering over the water that was always there for Solinje's dog.

Santekul did not underestimate his own powers. He was a herbalist, a hypnotist and an accomplished surgeon. His gifts were inherited; moreover they had been developed by teachers of the new world and he had worked and been respected in hospitals in South Africa, Europe and America.

But tonight he felt old and tired.

Like King Sol and the boy Solinje, those two symbols of the past and the future, he too felt a great need to fortify his depleted strength.

For the first time in his experience of a sacrificial ritual he felt diminished and sapped of strength, as if it were he who had undergone the blood-letting.

The snake, having slaked its thirst, returned to the body of the Witch-doctor in search of warmth. Santekul was glad of the creature. Its grace and beauty pleased him. It made no demands upon him; they suited one another. Sometimes he talked to it, although he knew the serpent to be deaf, a reptile without ears.

'We will sleep in this hut tonight,' he said. 'She is dead. But, as our ancestors prove to us, there is no such thing as death. The spirit is immortal. This hut is still alive with her spirit – an old wise spirit that has endured down the centuries right back to the days of the pagan deities and Greek philosophers.'

He decided that he must try a few more experiments himself with this plant that grew by the Big River, this hemlock.

Even the thought of it made him pleasantly drowsy.

Dr Santekul lay on Mrs Carpenter's divan and covered himself with her warm jet-blanket which he had appropriated after the ritual on the Rock.

He had partaken of the *muti* after the ritual, a physical act which required faith to make it potent. He had held that faith and had profited by the ceremony which, at that point, had been conducted by the Rain-Maker.

He had expected here, in Mrs Carpenter's hut, to feel his victim's antagonism and the need to overcome it. Instead, as he fell asleep, it was the boy, Solinje, who stood by his bed in a dream, the dog of no known make at his side. The child's eyes were innocent and without reproach.

When lightning struck the hut the snake slithered out into the storm while his master slept on under the burning thatch which rained its showers of sparks onto the hostage's splendid blanket.

The call came through to Kim Farrar at Judy's flat. It was ten-thirty. Rain drummed on the window-panes and blurred the view of city lights. It muted the endless roar of the night traffic and Judy cursed under her breath as she picked up the receiver.

'Kim Farrar? Just a moment, Desmond. I'll get him for you.'

'Kim? This is urgent! We want you here at the Embassy just as fast as you can make it within the bounds of safety. There's to be a press conference at midnight. H.E.'s with Brigadier Browne, the Director of Defence Forces and Press Liaison.'

'Good heavens! What has S.A.D.F. to do with Maud Carpenter?'

'A hell of a lot! A small South African border patrol – a sergeant in a jeep with a White and a Black corporal – have found someone they believe to be the "lady who was kidnapped at Marula Grove".'

'Alive?'

'No. We haven't got the full facts yet. But it seems the patrol took shelter from a storm. They discovered her on South African territory between the Big River and Marula.'

Suddenly Kim knew.

'In the baobab?'

'Yes. They reckoned she'd been dead about twenty hours at a rough guess. It's all very mysterious.' He sounded distraught. 'You understand I can't go into details now. The point is we need you here desperately. The whole matter has become a delicate diplomatic issue to be handled by the press with the utmost discretion. Hence H.E.'s conference tonight.'

'One more thing. Has Maud Carpenter been definitely identified?'

'Not yet. An army chopper's flying the body here to Pretoria, where the formalities will begin in earnest. Identification, post-mortem, an attempt to ascertain time, place and manner of death –'

'And who was responsible?'

'That may have to be hushed up.'

'Oh, God! Poor Janie! All right, Des, I'll be on my way at once. Please tell H.E. how shocked I am for all the family.'

He began to dress quickly while Judy slipped on a light woollen housecoat.

'I heard all that, Kim. It's horrible. The last hope gone. Can I make you some coffee? A drink?'

'Nothing. Just pray it's not Maud they've found.'

When he had gone she switched on her radio in time to hear the eleven o'clock News.

'On his return from Geneva this afternoon, Mr Abelard Cain, the popular young Director of Nyangreela's Hydro-Casino, left Jan Smuts Airport alone in his private helicopter. He was expected at Hydro-Casino this evening, but no word has been heard from him. However a helicopter similar to his own was seen to be struck by lightning over the high watershed of Nyangreela Park. A shepherd reports hearing a loud explosion as the lightning flash struck the chopper, after which it burst into flame and crashed in the forest. An extensive area of bush and timber was destroyed before a deluge of rain quenched the flames. As yet nothing as been found to identify the pilot or his passenger.'

Kim heard the same announcement in his car.

Poor devil, he thought. He knew too much. And the pilot's 'passenger'? Could that passenger have been the girl who'd made the necklace Abelard had worn so proudly that day at the cove when Old Man Baboon had watched them from his high ledge while 'Sea-Sprite' rocked in the cold sea – the very ocean from which the Rain-Maker had been supplied with water for her tribal rituals?

'Half-past-twelve,' said Mabel with yet another anxious glance at the clock. 'It's too much for your father, Janie. He hasn't had a let-up since he landed this afternoon. They must surely have finished their conference by now?'

Jane started. 'That's his step. Oh, Mabel, what are we going to hear next?'

A fire burned in the grate of the small morning-room Mabel regarded as her own. By day it was sunny and at night cosy when the Transvaal frost was silvering the lawn outside.

The Ambassador slumped into a high-backed chair and held out his hands to the welcome blaze. Jane fetched him a whisky and water and set it beside him. Then she sat at his feet, near Kirsty, who, as usual, monopolised the hearthrug.

'Have the others gone?' asked Mabel.

'Not yet. Brigadier Browne and Kim are still working out the final details for the media, while the Minister and Des are giving them all the assistance they can, using my directives as guide-lines. All that can be done for the present is under control. There are just a few extra things you and Janie have a right to be told.'

Jane took her father's hand and laid it against her cheek. The aroma of tobacco was strong on his skin. He'd been smoking too much as he did under stress.

'Go ahead, Daddy. Don't spare us. Just give us any facts we haven't already heard from Brigadier Browne.'

'I'll try. We've interviewed the patrol who found her. They were brought back to Pretoria in a fast military aircraft. Maud has been identified by Desmond and me. The cause of death has been established. Heart failure.'

His hand fell onto Jane's shoulder and grasped it gently. He felt her stiffen.

'Give us the truth, Daddy. All of it. Between you and me, only the truth is good enough. We both know that now. It must always be so.'

Mabel saw the strength return to her husband's face, given courage by the acceptance of the girl at his feet.

'Very well, then. As you already know, she was found in the hollow baobab. The sergeant in charge of the patrol described it in a strangely reverent way. He said, "It was as if the lady had been laid out very carefully in a little natural chapel." He took photographs. They could be pictures of a very exotic queen.'

He gave Jane the three flashlight colour prints. She rose and studied them under the standard-lamp, then passed them to Mabel in silence.

'They're almost beautiful,' said Mabel at last. 'But so strange! The beaded band round her brow, the cape that covers her. What does it all mean?'

'The mantle is cowhide, the best,' said Sir Hugh. 'The sort used by a person of great importance.'

Jane, still standing under the light, was pale to the lips.

'It's grotesque, some sort of masquerade. Black magic.'

She took the prints from Mabel with shaking fingers and put

them on the table by her father's chair. She sank onto the arm and felt his own surround her.

'Janie darling, look beyond the masquerade. Look at your grandmother's sleeping face and tell me what you see.'

Reluctantly she accepted the print he offered her at random. 'Look beyond the masquerade,' he had said. She made herself do so. Mabel watched the tense young face slowly relax and the colour return to her cheeks. At last Jane spoke.

'A trance, Daddy. A deep trance of peace. If only I had something of hers to touch, something belonging to her.'

'You have. There was a necklace with a little pouch that hung round her neck. The doctor at the mortuary removed it in Brigadier Browne's presence and gave it into his care. The Brigadier asked me to see that you received it. It was clearly intended for you.'

He drew it from his pocket and it lay, warm with life, in her palm. She longed to open the little purse, but that she must do later.

There was one more question she had to ask and the Ambassador knew that she would do so. Mabel, too, was ready for it. Jane held the necklace and the purse against her own breast like an amulet as she faced her father.

'Daddy, was she mutilated?'

He said steadily: 'Under that necklace was a perfect surgical incision in the shape of a star. Through the opening the operator had taken her heart. No other mark of violence had touched her. No sign of a struggle, not even a bruise.'

'Thank you, Daddy.'

Jane touched his thick grey hair with her lips. 'I'm going to bed now. Goodnight, Mabel.'

At the door she turned.

'I would like to see Desmond.'

'I will send him to your sitting-room,' said the Ambassador.

When Jane had closed the door behind her, Mabel lifted the receiver of the intercom and handed it to her husband.

When he gave it back to her, he held out his arms to her and she knew that at last the barriers between them were melting away.

'Des,' said Jane. 'Do you know what this little purse contains?'

'Brigadier Browne told me. He said it was a note for you from your grandmother and he thought perhaps it held a message for me too. He had to go through her things, Janie. There was very little. He saw how upset I was.'

'I understand.'

'This has been the longest day, darling. Do you want to read that message now, whatever it may be?'

'Stay with me while I do.'

He sat beside her on the small chintz couch, his arm about her as she opened the little purse and drew out the carefully folded doily that had once held pomegranates in a clay calabash.

Don't grieve, darling Janie. My surroundings are primitive but beautiful. I have found friendship here, respect, solitude without loneliness, and I have lost my heart to a little boy with a mongrel dog. Don't worry about 'Personal Problems'. I have learnt now that every story is only half a story. When you know *all* Ann's story, and your own, you will face your fruitful happy future with every right to its blessings.

Life here is close to nature and so, perhaps, to revelations. I am at peace.

Go well, my child, and may the man you love go with you.

Your Gran.